MICHELLE CELMER

VIRGIN PRINCESS, TYCOON'S TEMPTATION

D0125555

Silhouette®

Desire

Published by Silhouette Books

America's Publisher of Contemporary Romance

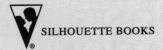

SILHOUETTE BOOKS
®

ISBN-13: 978-0-373-73039-1

VIRGIN PRINCESS, TYCOON'S TEMPTATION

Recycling programs
for this product may
not exist in your area.

Visit Silhouette Books at www.eHarlequin.com

Printed in U.S.A.

Books by Michelle Celmer

Silhouette Desire

Playing by the Baby Rules #1566
The Seduction Request #1626
Bedroom Secrets #1656
Round-the-Clock Temptation #1683
House Calls #1703
The Millionaire's Pregnant Mistress #1739
The Secretary's Secret #1774
Best Man's Conquest #1799
The King's Convenient Bride #1876
The Illegitimate Prince's Baby #1877
An Affair with the Princess #1900
The Duke's Boardroom Affair #1919
Royal Seducer #1951
The Oilman's Baby Bargain #1970
Christmas with the Prince #1979
Money Man's Fiancée Negotiation #2006
Virgin Princess, Tycoon's Temptation #2026

*Royal Seductions

MICHELLE CELMER

Bestselling author Michelle Celmer lives in southeastern Michigan with her husband, their three children, two dogs and two cats. When she's not writing or busy being a mom, you can find her in the garden or curled up with a romance novel. And if you twist her arm really hard you can usually persuade her into a day of power shopping.

Michelle loves to hear from readers. Visit her Web site, www.michellecelmer.com, or write her at P.O. Box 300, Clawson, MI 48017.

To my grandson, Cameron James Ronald

One

A genuine believer in fate and fairy tale romances, Princess Louisa Josephine Elisabeth Alexander knew that if she was patient, the man of her dreams would eventually come along. And as their eyes met across the crowded ballroom, beneath a canopy of red and white twinkling lights, shimmering silver tulle and pink, white and red heart-shaped balloons, she could swear she felt the earth move.

She just knew he was the one.

Her family would probably remind her that she'd felt that way about men before. Aaron would tease her and call her a hopeless romantic. Chris, the oldest, would just sigh and shake his head, as if to say, "Here we go again." Her twin sister Anne would probably sneer and call her naive. But this time it was different. Louisa was sure of it. She could *feel* it, like a cosmic tug at her soul.

He was the most intriguing, handsome and *tallest*

man—by several inches—at the charity event, which was what drew her attention to him in the first place. With raven hair, a warm olive complexion and striking features, he was impossible to miss.

Was he an Italian businessman, or a Mediterranean prince? Whoever he was, he was rich and powerful. She could tell by the quality of his clothing and the way he carried himself. Most people knew better than to openly stare at a member of the royal family, but this man gazed intently at her with dark, deep-set eyes, as though they already knew one another. Which she was sure they didn't. She definitely would have remembered him. Maybe he didn't realize she was royalty, although she would imagine the diamond encrusted tiara tucked within her upswept hair would be a dead giveaway.

Another woman might have waited for him to make the first move, or manufactured a scenario in which their paths accidentally crossed, but Louisa didn't believe in playing games. Much to the chagrin of her overly protective siblings. The youngest member of the royal family by a mere five minutes, and labeled as too trusting, Louisa was treated like a child. But contrary to what her family believed, not everyone was interested in her money and title, and those who were, were fairly easy to recognize.

She set her empty champagne glass on a passing server's tray and headed in his direction, the full skirt of her gown—in her customary shade of pink—swishing soundlessly as she crossed the floor. Never once did his eyes leave hers. As she approached, he finally lowered his gaze and bowed his head, saying in a voice as deep as it was smooth, "Her Highness is enchanting tonight."

Not a half-bad opening line, and he spoke with a

dialect not unlike her own. Almost definitely from Thomas Isle, so why didn't she recognize him? "You seem to have me at a disadvantage," she said. "You obviously know me, but I don't recall ever meeting you."

Most people, especially a stranger, would have at least offered an apology for staring, but this man didn't look like the type who apologized for *anything*. "That's because we've never met," he answered.

"I suppose that would explain it," she said with a smile.

Face-to-face, he was a little older than she'd guessed. Mid-thirties maybe—ten years or so her senior—but she preferred men who were older and more experienced. He was also much larger than she thought. The top of her head barely reached his chin. It wasn't just his height that was so imposing, either. He was big all over, and she would bet that not an ounce of it was fat. Even through his attire, he seemed to have the chiseled physique of a gladiator. She couldn't help noticing that he wasn't wearing a wedding ring.

This was, without a doubt, *fate*.

She offered a hand to shake. "Princess Louisa Josephine Elisabeth Alexander."

"That's quite a mouthful," he said, but she could see by the playful grin that he was teasing her.

He took her hand, cradled it within his ridiculously large palm, lifted it to his mouth and brushed a very gentle kiss across her skin. Did the ground beneath her feet just give a vigorous jolt, or was that her heart?

"And you are…?" she asked.

"Honored to meet you, Your Highness."

Either he had no grasp of etiquette, or he was being deliberately obtuse. "You have a name?"

His wry smile said he was teasing her again and she felt her heart flutter. "Garrett Sutherland," he said.

Sutherland? Why did that sound so familiar? Then it hit her. She had heard her brother speak of him from time to time, a landowner with holdings so vast they nearly matched those of the royal family. Mr. Sutherland was not only one of the richest men in the country, but also the most mysterious and elusive. He never attended social gatherings, and other than an occasional business meeting, kept largely to himself.

Definitely not the kind of man who would need her money.

"Mr. Sutherland," she said. "Your reputation precedes you. It's a pleasure to finally make your acquaintance."

"The pleasure is all mine, Your Highness. As you probably know, I don't normally attend events such as these, but when I heard the proceeds would benefit cardiac research, for your father's sake at the very least, I knew I had to make an appearance."

A testament to what a kind and caring man he must be, she thought. Someone she would very much like to get to know better.

His gaze left hers briefly to search the room. "I haven't seen the King tonight. Is he well?"

"Very well, under the circumstances. He wanted to make an appearance but he has strict orders from his doctor not to appear in public."

Louisa's father, the King of Thomas Isle, suffered from heart disease and had spent the past nine months on a portable bypass machine designed to give his heart an opportunity to heal and eventually work on its own again. Louisa took pride in the fact that it had been her idea to hold a charity ball in his honor. Usually her family wrote off her ideas as silly and idealistic, but for the first time in her life, they seemed to take her seriously. Although, when she had asked to be given the responsibility of planning the affair, they had hired a team of professionals instead. Baby steps, she figured. One of these days they would see that she wasn't the frail flower they made her out to be.

Across the ballroom the orchestra began playing her favorite waltz. "Would you care to dance, Mr. Sutherland?"

He arched one dark brow curiously. Most women would wait for the man to make the first move, but she wasn't most women. Besides, this was destiny. What could be the harm in moving things along a bit?

"I would be honored, Your Highness."

He held out his arm, and she slipped hers through it. As he led her through clusters of guests toward the dance floor, she half expected one of her overprotective siblings to cut them off at the pass, but Chris and his wife Melissa, enormously pregnant with triplets, were acting as host and hostess in their parents' absence. Aaron was glued to the side of his new wife, Olivia, a scientist who, when she wasn't in her lab buried in research, felt like a fish out of water.

Louisa searched out her sister Anne, surprised to find her talking to the Prime Minister's son, Samuel Baldwin, who Louisa knew for a fact was not on Anne's list of favorite people.

Not a single member of her family was paying attention to her. Louisa could hardly fathom that she was about to dance with a man without *someone* grilling him beforehand. He took her in his arms and twirled her across the floor, and they were blissfully alone—save for the hundred or so other couples dancing. But as he drew her close and gazed into her eyes, there was no one but them.

He held her scandalously close for a first dance—by royal standards anyhow—but it was like magic, the way their bodies fit and how they moved in perfect sync. The way he never stopped gazing into her eyes, as though they were a window into her soul. His were black and bottomless and as mysterious as the man. He smelled delicious, too. Spicy and clean. His hair looked so soft she wanted to run her fingers through it and she was dying to know how his lips would taste, even though she felt instinctively they would be as delicious as the rest of him.

When the song ended and a slower number began, he pulled her closer, until she was tucked firmly against the warmth of his body. Two songs turned to three, then four.

Neither spoke. Words seemed unnecessary. His eyes and the curve of his smile told her exactly what he was thinking and feeling. Only when the orchestra stopped to take a break did he reluctantly let go. He led her from the dance floor, and she was only vaguely aware that people were staring at her. At them. They probably wondered who this dark mysterious man was dancing with the Princess. Were they an item? She would bet that people could tell just by looking at them that they were destined to be together.

"Would you care to take a stroll on the patio?" she asked.

He gestured to the French doors leading out into the garden. "After you, Your Highness."

The air had chilled with the setting sun and a cool, salty ocean breeze blew in from the bluff. With the exception of the guards positioned at either side of the garden entrance, they were alone.

"Beautiful night," Garrett said, gazing up at the star-filled sky.

"It is," she agreed. June had always been her favorite month, when the world was alive with color and new life. What better time to meet the man of her dreams? Her soul mate.

"Tell me about yourself, Mr. Sutherland."

He turned to her and smiled. "What would you like to know?"

Anything. *Everything.* "You live on Thomas Isle?"

"Since the day I was born. I was raised just outside the village of Varie on the other side of the island."

The village to which he referred could only be described as quaint. Definitely not where you would expect to find a family of excessive means. Not that it mattered to her where he came from. Only that he was here now, with her. "What do your parents do?"

"My father was a farmer, my mother a seamstress. They're both retired now and living in England with my brother and his family."

It was difficult to fathom that such a wealthy and shrewd businessman was raised with such modest means. He had obviously done quite well for himself.

"How many siblings do you have?" she asked.

"Three brothers."

"Younger? Older?"

"I'm the eldest."

She wished, if only for a day or two, she could know what that felt like. To not be coddled and treated like a child. To be the person everyone turned to for guidance and advice.

A chilly breeze blew in from the bluff and Louisa shivered, rubbing warmth into her bare arms. They should go back inside before she caught a cold—with her father's condition it was important that everyone in the family stay healthy—but she relished this time alone with him.

"You're cold," he said.

"A little," she admitted, sure that he would suggest they head back in, but instead he removed his tux jacket and draped it over her shoulders, surrounding her in the toasty warmth of his body and the spicy sent of his cologne. What she really wanted, what she *longed* for, was for him to pull her into his arms and kiss her. She already knew that his lips would be firm but gentle, his mouth delicious. Heaven knows she had played the scene over in her mind a million times since adolescence, what the perfect kiss would be like, yet no man had ever measured up to the fantasy. Garrett would, she was sure of it. Even if she had to make the first move.

She was contemplating doing just that when a figure appeared in the open doorway. She turned to find that, watching them, with a stern look on his face, was her oldest brother, Chris.

"Mr. Sutherland," he said. "I'm so pleased to see that you've finally accepted an invitation to celebrate with us."

Garrett bowed his head and said, "Your Highness."

Chris stepped forward and shook his hand, but there was an undertone of tension in his voice, in his stance.

Did he dislike Garrett? Mistrust him? Or maybe he was just being his usual protective self.

"I see you've met the Princess," he said.

"She's a lovely woman," Garrett replied. "Although I fear I may have monopolized her time."

Chris shot her a sharp look. "She does have duties."

As princess it was her responsibility to socialize with *all* the guests, especially in her parents' absence, and duty was duty.

Another time and place. Definitely.

"Give me a minute, please," she asked her brother.

He grudgingly nodded and told Mr. Sutherland, "Enjoy your evening." Then he walked away.

Louisa smiled apologetically. "I'm sorry if he seemed rude. He's a little protective of me. My entire family is."

His smile was understanding. "If I had a sister so lovely, I would be, too."

"I suppose I should go back inside and mingle with the other guests."

His look said he shared her disappointment. "I understand, Your Highness."

She took off his jacket and handed it back to him. "I was wondering if you might like to be my guest for dinner at the castle."

A smile spread across his beautiful mouth. "I would like that very much."

"Are you free this coming Friday?"

"If not, I'll clear my schedule."

"We dine at seven sharp, but you can come a little early. Say, six-thirty?"

"I'll be there." He reached for her hand, brushing

another gentle kiss across her bare skin. "Good night, Your Highness."

He flashed her one last sizzling grin, then turned and walked back inside. She watched him go until he was swallowed up by the crowd, knowing that the next six days, until she saw him again, when she could gaze into the dark and hypnotizing depths of his eyes, would be the longest in her life.

Two

Garrett sipped champagne and strolled the perimeter of the ballroom, eyes on the object of his latest fascination. Everything was going exactly as planned.

"That was quite a performance," someone said from behind him, and he turned to see Weston Banes, his best friend and business manager, smiling wryly.

He pasted on an innocent look. "Who said it was a performance?"

Wes shot him a knowing look. He had worked with Garrett since he bought his first parcel of land ten years ago. He knew better than anyone that Garrett would have never attended the ball without some ulterior motive.

"I've hit a brick wall," Garrett told him.

Wes frowned. "I don't follow you."

"I now own every available parcel of commercial land that doesn't belong to the royal family, so there's only one thing left for me to do."

"What's that?"

"Take control of the royal family's land, as well."

A slow smile spread across Wes's face. "And the only way to do that is to marry into the family."

"Exactly." He had two choices, Princess Anne, who he'd commonly heard referred to as *The Shrew,* or Princess Louisa, the sweet, innocent and gullible twin. It was pretty much a no-brainer. Although, considering the way she'd looked at him, as responsive as she was to his touch, he wondered if she wasn't as sweet and innocent as her reputation claimed.

Wes shook his head. "This is ruthless, even for you. Anything to pad the portfolio, I guess."

This wasn't about money. He already had more than he could ever spend. This was about power and control. To marry the Princess, the monarchy would first have to assign him a title—most likely Duke—then he would be considered royalty. The son of a farmer and a seamstress becoming one of the most powerful men in the country. Who would have imagined? If he played his cards right, which he always did, someday he would control the entire island.

"We can discuss the details later," Garrett told him. "I wouldn't mind your input, seeing how this involves you, as well."

"This is really something coming from the man who swore he would never get married or have children," Wes said.

Garrett shrugged. "Sometimes a man has to make sacrifices."

"So, how did it go?"

"Quite well."

"If that's true, then why are you here, and she's way over there?"

His smile was a smug one. "Because I already got what I came for."

"I'm afraid to ask what that was."

Garrett chuckled. "Get your mind out of the gutter. I'm talking about an invitation to dinner at the castle."

His brows rose. "Seriously?"

"This Friday at six-thirty."

"Damn." He shook his head in disbelief. "You're good."

He shrugged. "It's a gift. Women can't resist my charm. Just ask your wife."

Wes turned to see Tia, his wife of five years, standing with a throng of society women near the bar. "I should probably intervene before she drinks her weight in champagne and I have to carry her out of here."

"You need to let her out more," Garrett joked.

"I wish," Wes said. Despite considerable means, Tia was the kind of nervous new mother who believed no one could care for their child as well as she and Wes, but he worked ridiculous hours and because of that she didn't get out very often. In fact, this was the first public function they had attended since Will's birth three months ago.

"Join us?" Wes asked, gesturing in his spouse's direction.

Garrett gave one last glance to the Princess, who was deep in conversation with a group of heads of state, then nodded and followed Wes to the bar. He already had a game plan in place. What he would say to her and what he wouldn't, when they would share their first kiss. The trick with a woman like her was to take it very slow.

He had little doubt that in no time, probably next Friday, he would have her eating out of the palm of his hand.

Louisa had been right.

It had been a murderously *long* week waiting for Friday to arrive, and when it finally did, the day seemed to stretch on for weeks. Finally, when she thought she couldn't stand another second of waiting, at six-thirty on the dot, a shiny black convertible sports car pulled up in front of the castle and Garrett unfolded himself from inside.

She watched from the library, surprised that someone of his means didn't have a driver, and wondering how such a big man fit into such a tiny vehicle. Maybe someday he would take her for a drive in it. With her bodyguards following close behind of course, because no member of the royal family was allowed to leave the castle unescorted. Especially not since the threats began late last summer.

Louisa peeked out from behind the curtain, watching as Garrett walked to the door. He looked so handsome and distinguished in a dark gray, pinstripe suit. And *tall*. She'd almost forgotten just how big he was.

Her brother Chris hadn't been happy about the short notice when she'd informed him this morning that she had invited Garrett for dinner. She knew though that if she'd told him sooner, the family would have teased and harassed her mercilessly all week.

As it was, everyone had managed to get their digs in this afternoon. Chris of course questioned Garrett's motives, as though no man would appreciate her for anything but her money and connections. Aaron voiced concern about the age difference—which, as Louisa had guessed, was just over ten years. Anne, who had been particularly cranky since the ball, warned her that a man like Garrett Sutherland was way out of her league and only interested in one thing. Louisa would love to know how Anne knew that when she didn't even know Garrett. Even her parents, who had been relying on Chris's judgment lately, were reserving their opinion. She wished, just this once, that everyone would mind their own business.

When Chris married an illegitimate princess, everyone just had to smile and go along with it for the good of the country, and when Aaron announced that he was going to marry an American scientist, an orphan who had not even a trace of royal blood, barely anyone voiced an objection. So what was the big deal about Louisa dating a rich and successful businessman?

She had checked up on him this week, purely out of curiosity of course, and though she hadn't been able to find too much information, none of it had been negative.

She was sure, though, that since her announcement this morning, Chris had ordered Randall Jenkins, their head of security, to dig up all the information he could find on Garrett. Louisa wasn't worried. She knew instinctively that he was a good person because she was an excellent judge of character.

The bell rang and she scurried over to the sofa to wait while Geoffrey, their butler, let Garrett in. She sat on the edge of the cushion and smoothed the wrinkles from the skirt of her pale pink sleeveless sundress, her heart pounding so hard it felt as though it might beat right through her chest.

Under normal circumstances she would have worn something a bit more conservative, like a business suit, for a dinner guest, but this was a first date and she wanted to look her best. Make a good first impression.

It seemed to take a millennium before the library door opened and Garrett strolled into the room. She rose to her feet to greet him.

Garrett wore his confidence like a badge of honor. So different from the cocky young royals she'd been introduced to in the past, who reeked of wealth and entitlement, as though their name alone afforded them everything their greedy and spoiled hearts desired.

Louisa and her siblings had been raised with wealth and privilege, but taught not to take anything for granted. Life, they had learned, especially since their father's illness, was fragile, and family was what mattered above all else.

Maybe it was wishful thinking, but she had the distinct feeling Garrett shared those values.

When he saw her standing there, a gorgeous smile curled his lips. He bowed his head and said, "Your Highness, a pleasure to see you again."

"I'm so glad you could make it," she replied, even though she'd never had a single doubt that he would show. What had happened between them on the dance floor had been magical and she was certain that they were destined to be together. Besides, his assistant had phoned hers this morning to confirm.

"Would you care for a drink, sir?" Geoffrey offered.

"Scotch, please," Garrett said, and his manners made Louisa smile. There was nothing she despised more than a man who treated the hired help with disrespect.

Especially Geoffrey, who had been with them since before Louisa was born and almost single-handedly kept the household running like clockwork.

"White wine, Your Highness?" Geoffrey asked her.

She nodded. "That would be lovely, thank you."

She gestured to the sofa and told Garrett, "Please, make yourself comfortable."

He settled onto the cushion, looking remarkably relaxed, as though he dined with royalty on a daily basis, when she knew for a fact that the charity ball had been the first time he had visited the castle under social circumstances. She sat at the opposite end, all but crawling out of her skin with excitement. When their drinks were poured, Geoffrey excused himself and they were *finally* alone. No family breathing down her neck, no bodyguards watching their every move.

"I was looking forward to my parents meeting you, but unfortunately they won't be joining us this evening."

"Your father isn't well?" he asked, looking concerned.

"He's going in for a procedure soon and has to stay in tip-top shape. The fewer people he's exposed to, the less likely he is to contract illnesses. His immune system is already compromised by the heart pump."

"Another time," he said. Was that his way of suggesting that he wanted to see her again? Not that she ever doubted he would. This was destiny.

It was still nice to hear the words out loud, to know what he was thinking.

"I'll warn you that tonight might feel more like the Spanish Inquisition than a dinner," she told him.

Garrett smiled. "I expected as much. I have nothing to hide."

"I Googled you," she admitted.

Her honesty seemed to surprise him. "Did you?"

"Earlier this week, although I didn't find much."

"There isn't much to find. I am a simple man, Your Highness. What some may even consider...boring."

She seriously doubted that. Everything about him intrigued her. He was so dark and serious, yet his smile was warm and inviting. She liked the way his eyes crinkled slightly in the corners when he smiled, and the hint of a dimple that dented his left cheek.

She opened her mouth to tell him that she would never consider a man like him boring, but before she could get the words out, her family appeared in the doorway. The entire lot of them.

Fantastic bloody timing. God forbid they let her have a little time alone with the man she planned to marry.

As everyone piled into the room, Garrett rose and Louisa stood to make the introductions.

"Garrett, I believe you already know my brothers, Prince Christian and Prince Aaron."

"A pleasure to see you again." Garrett bowed his head, then accepted a firm and brusque shake from each of them. Very businesslike, but with an undertone of possessiveness, a silent notification that he was being carefully assessed.

"This is my sister-in-law, Princess Melissa," Louisa said.

"Just Melissa," she added in the southern drawl she had adopted while living in the States. She shook his hand firmly and with purpose. For a southern belle, she didn't have a delicate or demure bone in her body. "It's a pleasure to finally meet you, Mr. Sutherland. I've heard so much about you."

"Please call me Garrett," he said. "I understand you're expecting. Congratulations."

"Kind of tough to miss at this point," she joked, laying a hand on her very swollen middle.

"I understand it will be soon."

"They prefer I make it to thirty-six weeks, so the babies' lungs have enough time to mature. Preterm labor is a possibility with multiples, but I can hardly imagine another month of this. I feel like an elephant."

"I've always believed there's nothing more beautiful than an expectant mother," Garrett said with genuine sincerity.

Melissa grinned widely and Louisa knew that he'd instantly won her over.

Aaron stepped forward and said, "This is my wife, Princess Olivia."

Liv smiled shyly, still unaccustomed to her role as a royal. A botanical geneticist, she was reserved and studious and would much rather be in her basement lab studying plant DNA than interacting with people. But she shook Garrett's hand and said, "Nice to meet you."

Anne, not waiting to be introduced, stepped forward and announced, "I'm Anne." She stuck out her hand, shaking Garrett's so firmly that Louisa worried she might challenge him to an arm wrestle.

What was her problem?

If Anne had been expecting a negative reaction from her confrontational introduction, she got the opposite.

"A pleasure to meet you, Your Highness," Garrett said with a smile, the picture of grace and etiquette, and Louisa all but beamed with pride. The situation couldn't be more tense or uncomfortable, yet he'd handled it with ease.

"I'll admit I was surprised when Louisa informed us this morning that you were joining us for dinner," Chris said, and Louisa wanted to punch him. Garrett had to be wondering why she would wait until this morning to tell them. She didn't want him to get the wrong idea, to think that she was ashamed of him or uncertain of her invitation.

Instead of appearing insulted, Garrett looked her way and flashed her that adorable, dimpled smile. "And I was a bit surprised when she asked." His eyes locked on hers with a look so warm and delicious she almost melted. "I could hardly believe I was lucky enough to draw the attention of the most beautiful woman in the room."

The honesty of his words and the admiration in his eyes warmed her from the inside out. The fact that he would speak so openly of his feelings for her, especially in front of her family, made her want to throw her arms around his neck and kiss him. But who wanted an audience for their first kiss?

Geoffrey appeared in the study door and announced, "Dinner is ready."

Melissa held out her arm for Chris to take. "Shall we?"

"Go ahead without me. I'd like to have a private word with our guest."

Louisa's heart nearly stopped. Why did Chris need to see him alone? She prayed he wouldn't say something embarrassing, or try to scare Garrett off. But if she made a fuss, it might only make things worse.

At Melissa's look of hesitance he added, "We'll only be a minute."

Louisa flashed Garrett an apologetic look, but he

just smiled, looking totally at ease as Melissa ushered everyone from the room.

With any luck, Garrett wouldn't decide that pursuing a princess was just too much hassle and bring an end to their first date before it even began.

Three

And so it begins, Garrett thought as the rest of the family walked, or in Melissa's case, waddled, from the room, leaving only himself and Prince Christian. He wondered if, had he been a royal, the Prince would feel this chat was necessary.

Well, it wouldn't be long before Garrett had a royal title, garnering him all of the respect he had earned. Though time wasn't an issue, he would still push for a quick engagement. The sooner they were married and settled, the sooner he could relax and begin enjoying all the fruits of his labor.

"Under normal circumstances it would be the King having this conversation with you," Chris said.

But the King wasn't well enough, so Garrett was stuck with the Crown Prince instead. He hadn't yet decided if that was a good or a bad thing. "I understand."

The Prince gestured to the sofa, and after Garrett

sat, Chris took a seat in the armchair across from him. "As a precaution, I had a thorough background check performed on you."

He had anticipated that, and as he had told Princess Louisa, he had nothing to hide. "Did they find anything interesting?"

"Actually, they didn't find much of anything at all. Though ruthless in your business practices, as far as I can tell you've always kept it legal and ethical, and you seem to be a fair employer. You donate a percentage of your income to worthwhile charities—most having to do with education for the underprivileged—and as far as any brushes with the law, you've never had so much as a parking ticket."

"You sound surprised."

"I would expect that a man so elusive might have something to hide."

"I certainly don't mean to be elusive," he said. "I simply lead an uncomplicated life. My work is my passion."

"It shows. Your accomplishments are quite impressive."

"Thank you."

The Prince paused for a second, as though he was uncomfortable with what he planned to say next. "While I see no clear reason to be concerned, I'm obligated to ask, on the King's behalf, what your intentions are regarding Princess Louisa."

It seemed ridiculous to Garrett that, at twenty-seven years old, Louisa wasn't allowed to make her own decisions regarding who she wanted to see socially. "Her Highness invited me to dinner and I accepted," he said.

The simplicity of his answer seemed to surprise the Prince. "That's it?"

"I admit I find your sister quite fascinating."

"Louisa is...special."

He said that as though that was an impediment, and Garrett felt an odd dash of defensiveness in her honor. Which was a little ridiculous considering he barely knew her.

"I've never met anyone quite like her," he told the Prince.

"She tends to be a bit naive when it comes to the opposite sex. Men have taken advantage of that."

Maybe if her family stopped sheltering her, she would learn not to be so gullible. However, that particular trait was working in his favor, so he could hardly complain. "Rest assured, I have nothing but the utmost respect for the Princess. I pride myself on being a very honorable man. I would never do anything to compromise her principles."

"I'm glad to hear it," Chris said. "But of course I will have to discuss the matter with the King."

"Of course, Your Highness."

The shadow of a smile cracked the serious expression. "We've known each other a long time, Garrett. Call me Chris."

With that request Garrett knew he was as good as in. Chris needing to speak with his father was merely a formality at this point. "I'm very much looking forward to getting to know you better," Garrett told him.

"As am I." Chris paused, his expression darkening, and said, "However, if you did take advantage of my sister, the consequences would be...unfortunate."

The fact that Garrett didn't even flinch seemed to

impress Chris. Still, Garrett was going to have to be very cautious while he courted Louisa.

Chris rose from his chair and said, "Shall we join the others?"

Garrett stood and followed him to the dining room. The first course was just being served, and as soon as they entered the room, Louisa shot from her seat and gestured him to the empty chair beside her.

When they were seated again, she leaned close to him and whispered, "I'm so sorry he did that. I hope he wasn't too hard on you."

He gave her a reassuring smile. "Not at all."

If he thought the worst was over, he realized quickly that it had only begun. He barely had a chance to taste his soup before Anne launched into the inquisition portion of the meal.

"I understand your father was a farmer," she said, her tone suggesting that made him inferior somehow.

It had only been a matter of time before someone broached the subject of his humble beginnings, but he wasn't ashamed of his past. He was instead very proud of his accomplishments. Although for the life of him he never understood why his parents hadn't strived to better themselves. Why they settled for a life barely a step above poverty when they could have done so much more for themselves and their sons.

"All of his life," Garrett told her. "My earliest memories are of working beside him in the fields."

"Yet you didn't follow in his footsteps," Anne noted, her words sounding an awful lot like an accusation. Much the way his father had sounded when Garrett had informed him that he planned to leave the island to attend college.

"No, I didn't. I wanted an education."

"How did your father feel about that?"

"Anne," Louisa said, plainly embarrassed by her sister's behavior.

"What?" Anne asked, her innocent look too manufactured to be genuine. He wasn't sure if she was jealous of Louisa, or simply being difficult because she could. If there was one thing Garrett knew for sure, he'd definitely chosen the right sister. Had he picked Anne, he would be asking for a life of misery.

"Stop being so nosy," Louisa said.

Anne shrugged. "How else can we get to know Mr. Sutherland?"

"Please call me Garrett," he told Anne. "And in answer to your question, my father wasn't at all happy with me. He expected me to take over the farm when he retired. I wanted to do something more with my life."

"Which you certainly have," Chris said, and maybe Garrett was imagining things, but he almost sounded impressed.

"If there's one thing I've learned," Garrett said, "it's that you can't live your life to please other people." He glanced over at Louisa, catching her eye for emphasis. "You have to follow your heart."

"I believe that, too," Olivia said. She reached over and placed a hand on her husband's arm. "Aaron is starting back to school in the fall. Premed."

"I'd heard that," Garrett said. He made it his business to know everything about his stiffest competition. Aaron's leaving the family business would create the convenient opening he required to insinuate himself inside.

"He's going to be a brilliant doctor," Olivia said,

beaming with pride. She was a plain woman, very young and unassuming, but pretty when she smiled… and quite the brilliant scientist from what he understood. The previous autumn, an unidentifiable blight potentially threatened all the crops on the island. The effects would have been devastating on the export trade, the main source of income for the country, and Olivia had been hired by the royal family to find an eco-friendly cure.

"I've heard that your own brilliance saved the livelihood of every landowner in the country," Garrett told her. "Myself included."

Olivia grinned shyly and blushed. It would seem that he had won over at least three-quarters of the females at the table. Anne seemed a lost cause at this point. Chris and Aaron, he wasn't sure about, but it looked promising. Now it was time for a change of subject, and he'd done his research.

"I understand you spent quite a lot of time in the States," Garrett said to Melissa.

"I was born on Morgan Isle but raised in New Orleans," she told him.

"A lovely city," he commented.

"You've been there?"

He nodded. "Several times in fact. For business. Terrible what happened during Katrina."

"It was. I started a foundation to fund the rehabilitation of the city."

"I had no idea. I'd love to make a donation."

Melissa smiled. "That would be lovely, thank you."

"I'll have a check sent round next week."

"What other places have you visited?" Louisa asked him, and they launched into a conversation about traveling abroad, and everyone's favorite vacation spot.

Garrett was pleasantly surprised to find that, with the exception of Anne, they were a friendly bunch, and not nearly as uptight as he'd expected. The tone of the conversation was not unlike those of his youth, when his family gathered for supper. In fact, by the time dessert was served, Garrett realized that he was actually enjoying himself.

Louisa didn't say much, but instead spent most of her time gazing up at him, seemingly mesmerized by every word that passed his lips.

After dinner, Chris pushed back from the table and asked Garrett, "Up for a friendly game of poker? We play every Friday evening."

Before he could answer, Louisa said, "Garrett and I are taking a walk in the garden." Which he took as his clue to decline their offer, when the truth was he would much rather play cards than take a leisurely stroll, but securing his position with Louisa took precedence for now.

"Maybe some other time," he told Chris.

"Of course." Chris turned to Louisa, his expression serious, and said, "Not too far, and I want you inside before sundown."

"I know," Louisa replied, sounding exasperated, and Garrett didn't blame her. He knew her family kept a tight grip on the reins, but telling a woman of twenty-seven that she couldn't stay out past dark bordered on the absurd.

Louisa slipped her arm through his and smiled up at him. "Ready?"

He thanked her family for dinner, then let Louisa lead him through the castle and out onto a patio that opened up into acres of lush flower gardens. The evening was a warm one, but a cool breeze blew in from the bluff.

She kept a firm grip on his arm as they started down the path, as though she feared the instant they were in the clear he might run for his life.

"I'm really sorry about my family," she said, looking apologetic. "As you probably noticed, they treat me like a child."

"They are quite...*protective*."

"It's humiliating. They think I'm naive."

Maybe they weren't so far off the mark, he thought wryly. She was unsophisticated enough to fall for his charms without question or doubt. Not that he would ever mistreat her, or compromise her honor. She would never suffer as his wife.

"I'm sure they mean well," he told her. "I imagine it would be much worse if they didn't care at all."

"I guess you're right," she conceded. "But since the threats started they've been a lot worse than usual. They think everyone I meet is a spy or something."

"I had seen something on the news about the security being breached in your father's hospital suite in London. I understand no one was able to identify the suspect from the surveillance footage."

"He calls himself the Gingerbread Man."

"Seriously?"

"Strange, I know. It started last summer with e-mail. He hacked into our computer system and sent threatening messages to us from our own accounts. They were all twisted versions of nursery rhymes."

"Nursery rhymes?" That didn't sound very threatening to him.

"Mine said, 'I love you, a bushel and a peck. A bushel

and a peck, and a noose around your neck. With a noose around your neck, you will drop into a heap. You'll drop into a heap and forever you will sleep.'" She looked up at him with a wry smile and said, "I memorized it."

On second thought, that was rather ominous. "What were the others?"

"I don't remember them word for word, but the common theme was burning alive."

Ouch. No wonder the family was being so cautious.

"At first we thought it was just an elaborate prank, until he managed to slip through castle security and get on the grounds. They think he scaled the bluff."

That explained the seemingly excessive security the night of the ball. "Was anyone harmed?"

"No, but he left a note. It said, 'Run, run, as fast as you can. You can't catch me. I'm the Gingerbread Man.' That's how we learned his name. We haven't heard anything from him lately, but that doesn't mean he's stopped. Things will be quiet for a while, then just when we think that he's given up, he'll leave another note somewhere or send an untraceable e-mail. He sent a gift basket full of rotten fruit for New Year's, then he sent flowers for Melissa and Chris congratulating them on the pregnancy. *Weeks* before the official announcement was made. He even knew that they were having triplets."

"Sounds like someone on the inside."

"We thought so, too, but everyone checked out."

At least her family's protectiveness made a bit more sense now. He just hoped it didn't interfere with his plans. It could be difficult courting a woman who wasn't allowed to leave her home.

"Enough about my family drama," she said, waving

the subject away like a pesky insect. "What is your family like?"

"Simple," he said, then quickly added, "Not intellectually. But they prefer to live a...*humble* lifestyle." One that didn't include him.

"What do your brothers do?"

"Two own a business together in England. They sell farming equipment. My youngest brother is something of a...wanderer. Last I heard he was working a cattle ranch in Scotland."

"I'd like to meet them," she said, with an eagerness that surprised him. "Maybe they could all come to the castle for a visit."

Considering he was trying to impress the royal family, that probably wouldn't be wise. "I'm not so sure that would be a good idea."

She frowned. "You're not ashamed of them?"

Once again, her directness surprised him. "I'm afraid it's quite the opposite."

Her eyes widened. "They're ashamed of *you?*"

"Maybe not ashamed, but they're not very pleased with the path I chose."

"How is that possible? Look how well you've done. All that you've accomplished. How can they not be proud?"

He'd asked himself that same question a million times, but had long ago given up trying to understand their reasoning. He no longer cared what they thought of him. "It's...complicated."

She patted his arm. "Well, I think you're amazing. The instant I saw you I knew you were special."

He could see that she truly meant it, and in an odd way he wished he could say the same of her. He was sure that Louisa was very special in her own right, and maybe someday he would learn to appreciate that.

"Tell me the truth," she said. "Did my family scare you off?"

He could see by her expression that she was genuinely concerned, but he was a man on a mission. It would take a lot more than a grilling by her siblings to get in his way.

He gave her arm a squeeze. "Absolutely not."

Her smile was one of relief. "Good. Because I really like you, Garrett."

Never had he met a woman so forward with her feelings, so willing to put herself out on a limb. He liked that about her, and at the same time it made him uncomfortable. He was taught by his father that showing affection made a man weak. If he loved his sons, his father never once said so.

But Garrett had the feeling that if he was going to make this relationship work, he was going to have to learn to be more open with his feelings. At least until he had a royal title and Louisa had a ring on her finger.

He smiled and said, "The feeling is mutual, Your Highness."

Four

Louisa gazed up at Garrett, looking so sweet and innocent. So...*pure*. He felt almost guilty for deceiving her.

"I think at this point it would be all right for you to call me Louisa," she said.

"All right, Louisa."

"Can we speak frankly?"

"Is there ever a time when you don't?"

Her cheeks blushed a charming shade of pink and she bit her lip. "Sorry. I have this terrible habit of saying everything that's on my mind. It drives everyone crazy."

"Don't apologize. It's a welcome change. Most women play games." Unless this was some sort of game she was playing. But his instincts told him that she didn't have a manipulative bone in her body.

"You should know that I'm not looking for a temporary

relationship. I want to settle down and have a family."
She stopped walking and looked up at him. "I need to
know that you feel the same. That you're not just playing
the field."

"I'm thirty-seven years old, Louisa. I think I've played
the field long enough."

"In that case, there's something else I should probably
mention."

Why did he sense that he wasn't going to like this?

"We should talk about children."

She certainly didn't pull any punches, although oddly,
he was finding that he liked that about her. "What about
them?"

"I want a big family."

He narrowed his eyes at her. "How big?"

The grip on his arm tightened, as though she was
worried he might try to make a run for it. "At least six
kids. Maybe more."

For a second he thought she might be joking, or testing
him, then he realized that she was dead serious.

Six kids? Bloody hell, no wonder she was still single.
Who in this day and age wanted that many children?
He'd never felt the desire or need to have one child, much
less half a dozen of them! Marrying a royal, he knew at
least one heir would be expected. Maybe two. But *six?*

Despite his strong feelings on the matter, he could
see by her expression that this was not a negotiable point
for Louisa and he chose his next words very carefully.
"I'll admit that I've never given any thought to having a
family that large, but anything is possible."

A bright and relieved smile lit her entire face and he
felt an undeniable flicker of guilt, which he promptly
shook off. This was business. Once they were married,

he would lay down the law and insist that two children at most would be plenty and she would eventually learn to live with that. Or maybe, after the first child or two, she would change her mind anyway. He'd seen the way his parents struggled with a large family, the emotional roller coaster rides. Who would want to subject themselves to that?

Louisa gazed up at him, a dreamy look on her face. "It would be okay if you kissed me now," she said, then added, "If you want to."

Oh, he wanted to. So much that it surprised him a little. The idea had been to wait until their second date before he kissed her, to draw out the anticipation. Did she intend to derail each one of his carefully laid plans? "Are you sure that's what you want?" he asked.

"Just because my family treats me like a child, that doesn't mean I am one."

There was nothing childish about her, which she proved by not even waiting for him to make the first move. Instead, she reached up, slid her hands behind his neck, pulled him down to her level and kissed him. Her lips were soft but insistent, and she smelled fantastic. Delicate and feminine.

Though he had intended to keep it brief, to take things slowly, he felt himself being drawn closer, as though pulled by an invisible rope anchored somewhere deep inside his chest. His arms went around her and when his fingers brushed her bare back, what felt like an electric shock arced through his fingers. Louisa must have felt it, too, because she whimpered and curled her fingers into the hair at his nape. He felt her tongue, slick and warm against the seam of his lips and he knew he had to taste her, and when he did, she was as sweet as candy.

He was aware that this was moving too far, too fast, but as she leaned in closer, pressing her body against his, he felt helpless to stop her. Never had the simple act of kissing a woman aroused him so thoroughly, but Louisa seemed to put her heart and soul, her entire being, into it.

To him, self-control was a virtue, but Louisa seemed to know exactly which buttons to push. Not at all what he would have expected from a woman rumored to be so sweet and innocent. Which had him believing that she really wasn't so sweet and innocent after all.

Her hands slipped down his shoulders and inside his jacket. She stroked his chest through his shirt and that was all he could take. He broke the kiss, breathless and bewildered, his heart hammering like mad.

Louisa expelled a soft shudder of breath and rested her head against his chest. "Now *that* was a kiss."

He couldn't exactly argue. Although the whole point of this visit had been to prove to her family that his intentions were pure, yet here he was, practically mauling her out in the open, where anyone could see. If someone *was* watching, he hoped they hadn't failed to notice that she'd made the first move and he'd been the one to put on the brakes.

She nuzzled her face to his chest, her breath warm through his shirt. He curled his hands into fists, to keep from tangling them through her hair, from drawing her head back and kissing her again. He wanted to taste her lips and her throat, nibble at her ears. He wanted to put his hands all over her.

"It probably isn't proper to say this," Louisa said, "but I can't wait to see you naked."

Bloody hell. He backed away and held her at arm's

length, before he did something really stupid like drag her into the bushes and have his way with her. "Do you ever *not* say what's on your mind?"

"I just gave you the censored version," she answered with an impish grin. "Would you like to know what I'm really thinking?"

Of course he would, but this was not the time or place. "I'll use my imagination." He glanced up at the darkening sky and said, "It's getting late. I should get you back inside."

"Lest I turn into a pumpkin," she said with a sigh and took his hand, as naturally as if they had known each other for years, and they walked down the path toward the castle.

"I had a good time tonight," he said.

"Me, too. Although I get the feeling that I'm not quite what you expected."

"No, you're not. You're more intriguing and compelling than I could have imagined."

As she smiled up at him, he realized that was probably the most honest thing he'd said all night.

Louisa stood in the study, watching as Garrett's car zipped down the drive, until the glow of his taillights disappeared past the front gate.

She sighed and rested her forehead against the cool glass. This had been, by far, one of the best nights of her life. Kissing Garrett had been…magical. Even if she had been the one to make the first move. Later, when he had kissed her goodbye, it was so sweet and tender she nearly melted into a puddle on the oriental rug.

He was definitely the one.

"He's using you."

Louisa whipped around to find Anne leaning in the study doorway, arms folded across her chest, her typical grumpy self. Typical for the last week or so, anyway.

"Why would you think that?" she asked.

"Because that's what men like him do. They use women like us. They feed us lies, then toss us aside like trash."

Louisa knew that, like herself, Anne hadn't had the best luck with men, but that reasoning was harsh, even for her. "Are you okay, Anne?"

"He's going to hurt you."

Louisa shook her head. "Garrett is different."

"How do you know that?"

"How do *you* know that he isn't?"

Anne sighed and shook her head, as though she pitied her poor, naive sister. Louisa would have been upset, but she knew that attacking her was Anne's way of working through her own anger. Not that she didn't get a little tired of being her sister's punching bag.

"I can take care of myself," Louisa told her.

Anne shrugged, as though she didn't care one way or another. Which she must, or she wouldn't have said anything in the first place. "Don't say I didn't warn you."

"Did something happen to you?" Louisa asked, and she could swear she saw a flicker of pain before Anne carefully smothered it with a look of annoyance.

"You think that just because I don't like Garrett, something is wrong with *me?*"

"You can talk to me, Anne. I want to help."

"You're the one who needs help if you think that man really has feelings for you." With one last pathetic shake of her head, Anne turned and left. Her sister was obviously hurting, and Louisa felt bad about it, but she wished Anne would stop trying to drag Louisa down with her. Why couldn't Anne just be happy for her for once?

Maybe she was jealous. Maybe Anne wanted Garrett for herself. Or maybe, like Louisa, she wanted someone to love her, to see her for who she really was. Even though Anne could be a real pain in the neck sometimes, deep down there was a sweetness about her, a tender side, and she was loyal to the death to the ones that she loved.

"You'll meet someone, too," Louisa whispered to the empty doorway, knowing with all her heart that it was true. Even though Anne was a little pessimistic and occasionally cranky, there was a man out there who would appreciate all her gifts and overlook her faults. He would love her for who she was, just the way Garrett would love Louisa.

Worried for her sister, she started out the door, intending to collect her Shih Tzu, Muffin—who had spent the afternoon with his groomer and behaviorist— and tell him all about her day, but she ran into Chris in the foyer.

"Poker game over already?" she asked. Typically they played well past eleven. Louisa didn't play cards, unless you counted War and Solitaire, but occasionally she liked to sit and watch them.

"Melissa was tired and Liv wanted to get back to the lab. Some new research project she's working on. I assume your evening was a success."

She smiled and nodded.

"Have you got a minute?"

"Actually, I was just on my way to get Muffin."

His expression darkened. "I suppose you heard what

your little mutt did to the pillows on the library sofa.
There was stuffing everywhere."

She cringed. "Yes. Sorry."

"The day before that it was Aaron's shoes."

"I know. I offered to replace them."

"He's a menace."

"He just wants attention."

"What he's going to get is a nice doghouse in the
gardens."

Even if she thought Chris was serious, that wouldn't
work either because every time Muffin was let outside
unsupervised he made a run for it.

"I'll keep a closer eye on him," she promised. "What
did you want to talk about?"

"Let's go in the study."

She couldn't tell if this would be a good talk, or a
bad talk. But she had the sneaking suspicion that it had
something to do with Garrett.

Louisa sat on the sofa while Chris fixed himself a
drink. In preparation for his role as future King, Chris
had always been the most responsible and aggressive
sibling. He honored the responsibility, oftentimes to his
own personal detriment. Still it surprised and impressed
Louisa, since having to take their father's place while he
was ill, how effortlessly Chris had slipped into his place
and taken over his responsibilities. She had no doubt that
if, God forbid, their father didn't recover, Chris would
make a fine king.

But she had every confidence that their father would
make a full recovery. He simply *had* to.

"I want you to know," Chris said, his back to her,
"I didn't appreciate you waiting until this morning to
announce that you had invited Garrett to dinner."

So he'd asked her here to scold her. Wonderful. "Can you really blame me? Had I said anything earlier I never would have heard the end of it."

He turned to her, took a swallow of his drink, then said, "You could have been putting the family in danger."

She rolled her eyes. "You say that like you haven't known Garrett for years. If he was dangerous, I'm sure we'd have heard about it a long time ago."

"You still have to follow the rules. We've all had to make sacrifices, Louisa."

As if she didn't know that. If they didn't treat her like a child, she would have been more forthcoming. This was more her siblings' fault than hers. They drove her to it. Sometimes she just got tired of being the obedient princess.

"I'm assuming that he must have checked out," she guessed, "or he never would have made it through the front gate."

"Yes, he did."

"I knew he would, and I didn't need a team of security operatives to tell me."

He shook his head, as though she was a hopeless cause. He crossed the room and sat on the sofa beside her. "I had a talk with Father about this earlier today, regarding his wishes concerning the matter."

Louisa held her breath. If the King disapproved of a man she wanted to date, she would be forbidden. Those were the rules. "And?"

"He told me to use my discretion."

Louisa wasn't sure if that was a good or a bad thing. At least she knew their father would be fair. Would Chris forbid her to see Garrett to teach her a lesson?

This was probably something she should have considered when she waited until the last second before telling Chris about Garrett's visit.

"And what did you decide?" she asked, flashing him the most wide-eyed and hopeful look she could manage.

He regarded her sternly for a moment, then a grin tipped up the corner of his mouth. "It's clear that you have feelings for the man. Of course you can see him."

She let out an excited squeal and threw her arms around Chris, hugging him so hard that his drink nearly sloshed onto the sofa. "Thank you! Thank you!"

"You're welcome," he said with a chuckle. *"However…"*

Oh boy, here came the conditions. She sat back and braced herself.

"No more stunts like you pulled this morning."

She shook her head. "Never. I promise. I swear, it won't happen again."

"In addition, you will not leave the premises without a minimum of two bodyguards, and I need at least two days' advance notice before you visit any sort of public place or attend a function. No exceptions, or I will not hesitate to place you on indefinite house arrest."

Inconvenient, but definitely doable. "No problem."

"And please, let's try not to give the press anything to salivate over. With Father's health, the last thing the family needs is more gossip and rumors."

She refrained from rolling her eyes. Now he was being silly. "Honestly, Chris, have I *ever* been one to create a scandal?"

"It's not necessarily you I'm concerned about."

"You don't have to worry about Garrett, either. He's

a complete gentleman. So much so that when it came to kissing, I had to make the first move."

Chris cringed. "I really didn't need to know that. I'm counting on you to be…diplomatic."

Diplomatic? He made it sound as though she and Garrett were forming a business partnership. Besides, she knew for a fact that Chris hadn't been very "diplomatic" when he was first seeing Melissa. They couldn't seem to keep their hands off each other.

What he was really saying was that he expected her to live up to her reputation as the innocent and pure princess. Eventually her family was going to have to accept that she was a woman, not a child.

If only he knew what went on in her head, how curious she was about sex and eager to experiment. Most modern women didn't make it to twenty-seven with their virginity intact. He would probably drop in a dead faint if he knew about all of the reading she had done online about sex. When it came to intimacy, boy, was she ready. It was all she'd been able to think about since she had danced with Garrett on Saturday night.

"You don't have to worry about me or Garrett," she assured him and left it at that, and Chris looked relieved to have the subject closed.

"I want you to know that I like Garrett," he added.

"But…?"

"No buts. I think you and he would be a good match."

She eyed him skeptically. "Even though he isn't royal?"

"Liv isn't a royal," he reminded her.

True. Liv was an orphan from the States who didn't even know who her parents were, but there was always that double standard. A prince could get away with marrying a commoner. A princess on the other hand was held to a higher standard. She imagined that Garrett's money was probably his only saving grace. She would never be allowed to date a man of modest means.

"Given his background," Chris continued, "Garrett would be the perfect choice to take over Aaron's position now that he's going back to school. If you marry him, that is."

Oh, she would. The fact that he was already making plans to include Garrett in the family business was more than she could have hoped for. "I think that's a wonderful idea!"

"However," he added sternly, "I don't want you to think this means you should rush into anything."

How could she rush fate? Either it was or it wasn't meant to be. Time was irrelevant. Besides, Chris was one to talk. He'd asked Melissa to marry him after only two weeks. Of course, at the time, he'd expected nothing more than an arranged, loveless marriage. Boy, did he get more than he'd bargained for. But destiny was like that. And there was no doubt that he and Melissa were meant for one another.

Just like Louisa and Garrett.

She pictured them a year from now, married and blissfully happy, hopefully with their first baby on the way. Or maybe even born already. She would very much like to conceive on her honeymoon. What could be a more special way to celebrate the union of their souls than to create a new life? Some women dreamed of a career, and others liked to travel. Some spent their lives donating their time to charitable causes. All Louisa had ever wanted was to be a wife and mother. Archaic as some believed it to be, it was her ultimate dream. A man to cherish her, children to depend on her. Who could ask for more?

"By the way," Chris said. "Melissa and I are planning to go sailing Sunday."

"Is she allowed to do that so close to her due date?"

"As long as she takes it easy and stays off her feet. We figure we should get in as much time on the water before the babies come. You're welcome to join us. Garrett, too, if you'd like to invite him."

Her parents were leaving for England on Sunday morning for testing on her father's heart pump, and Anne was going with them. If Chris and Melissa were going to be gone, too, that would mean that she and Garrett could have some time alone, without her entire family watching over their shoulders. She wondered if there was any way she could get rid of Aaron and Liv, as well.

"Maybe next time," she told Chris. "I already have plans."

At least, she would have plans, just as soon as she called Garrett and invited him over.

Five

Garrett had just walked in the door of his town house when his cell phone rang. He looked at the display and saw that it was Louisa's personal line. When they had exchanged numbers earlier, he hadn't expected a call quite this soon. In fact, he'd just assumed he would be the one calling her.

It shouldn't have surprised him that she wouldn't let him make the next move. This so-called shy and innocent Princess seemed to have everyone snowed, because as far as he could tell, she didn't have a shy bone in her body. As for innocence, she certainly didn't act like an inexperienced virgin.

When he answered, she asked, "I'm not bothering you, am I?"

"Of course not." He dropped his keys and wallet on the kitchen counter then shrugged out of his jacket and draped it over the back of a chair. "I just walked in the door."

"I wanted to tell you again what a wonderful time I had this evening."

"I did, too." Things were progressing even more quickly than he'd hoped.

"I was wondering what you're doing Sunday afternoon. I thought you might like to come over."

He chuckled. "I suppose it's too much to expect that I might get to ask *you* on a date."

"Am I being too forward?" she asked, sounding worried.

"No, not at all. I like a woman who knows what she wants."

"I just wanted to catch you before you made other plans."

"If I'd made other plans, I would cancel them. And in answer to your question, I would very much like to come over. If it's all right with your family, that is."

"Of course it is. They love you."

That must have meant he'd passed the initiation. Not that he ever doubted he would. It was just nice to know that he'd scaled the first major obstacle.

"I thought maybe we could have a picnic," Louisa suggested. "Out on the bluff, overlooking the ocean."

"Just the two of us?"

"My parents and Anne will be leaving for England, and Chris and Melissa are going sailing. Liv will probably be tied up in the lab and lately Aaron has been down there assisting her. And as long as I stay on the grounds I don't need security at my heels, so we'll be alone."

He didn't miss the suggestive lilt in her tone, and

wondered what she expected they might be doing, other than picnicking that is.

"Muffin will be there, too, of course," she added.

"Muffin?"

"My dog. You would have met him today, but he was with the groomer and then his behaviorist. He's a Shih Tzu."

So, Muffin was one of those small yappy dogs that Garrett found overwhelmingly annoying. He preferred real dogs, like the shepherds and border collies they kept on the farm. Intelligent dogs with a brain larger than a walnut.

"He can be a bit belligerent at times," Louisa said, "but he's very sweet. I know you'll love him."

"I'm sure I will," he lied, and reminded himself again that this relationship would require making adjustments. It was just one more issue he could address after they were married.

The front bell rang and Garrett frowned. He wasn't expecting anyone. Who would make a social call this late?

"Was that your door?" Louisa asked.

"Yes, but I'm not expecting anyone."

"Could it be a lady friend perhaps?" Her tone was light, but he could hear an undercurrent of concern.

"The only woman in my life is you, Your Highness," he assured her, and could feel her smile into the phone.

The bell rang again. Whoever it was, they were bloody well impatient.

"I won't keep you," she said.

"What time would you like me there Sunday?"

"Let's say 11:00 a.m. We can make a day of it."

"Sounds perfect," he said, even though he'd never really been the picnicking type. He would much rather take her out to eat—preferably at the finest restaurant in town—but the heightened security was going to make dating a challenge.

They said their goodbyes and by the time Garrett made it to the door, the bell rang a third time. "I'm coming," he grumbled under his breath. He pulled the door open, repressing a groan when he saw who was standing there.

"What, you're not happy to see your baby brother?"

Not at all, in fact, but he did his best not to look too exasperated. "Last I heard you were working a cattle ranch in Scotland."

Ian shrugged and said, "Got bored. Besides, I have something big in the works. A brilliant plan."

In other words, he was let go and had formulated some new get-rich-quick scheme. One that, like all his other brilliant plans, would undoubtedly crash and burn.

"Aren't you going to invite me in?" Ian asked with forced cheer, but the rumpled clothes, long hair and the week's worth of beard stubble said this was anything but a friendly social call.

Letting Ian in was tantamount to inviting a vampire into the house. He had a gift for bleeding dry his host both emotionally and financially and an annoying habit of staying far past his welcome.

It was hard to believe that he was once the sweet little boy Garrett used to sit on his knee and read to, then tuck into bed at night. For the first eight years of Ian's life, he was Garrett's shadow.

"Mum and Dad turn you away?" Garrett asked, and

he could see by Ian's expression that they had. Not that Garrett blamed them.

The cheery facade fell and Ian faced him with pleading eyes, looking tired and defeated. "Please, Garrett. I spent my last dime on a boat to the island and I haven't had a proper meal in days."

Or a shower, guessing by the stench, and it was more likely that he'd conned his way to the island than paid a penny for passage. But he looked so damned pathetic standing there. Despite everything, Ian was still his brother. His family. The only family who would bother to give him the time of day.

Knowing he would probably regret it later, Garrett moved aside so his brother could step into the foyer. The cool evening air that followed him inside sent a chill down Garrett's back and when Ian dropped his duffel on the floor, a plume of dust left a dirty ring on the Italian ceramic tile. He would consider it a bad omen if he believed in that sort of thing.

"Spacious," Ian said, gazing around the foyer and up the wide staircase to the second floor. "You've done well for yourself."

"Don't touch anything." Things had a mysterious habit of finding their way into Ian's pockets and disappearing forever. "And take off your boots. I don't want you trailing mud on my floors."

"Could I trouble you for a shower?" Ian asked as he kicked off his boots, revealing socks so filthy and full of holes they barely covered his feet.

"You can use the one in the spare bedroom." It was the room that possessed the least valuable items. "Up the stairs, first door on the right. I'll fix something to eat."

Ian nodded, grabbed his duffel and headed up the

stairs. Garrett considered wiping up the dust on the floor, but there would probably be more where that came from, so he decided to take care of it in the morning after Ian was gone. He walked to the kitchen instead and put a kettle on for tea, then rummaged through the icebox to see what leftovers his housekeeper had stashed there. He found a glass dish with a generous portion of pot roast, baked red skin potatoes and buttered baby carrots from last night's dinner.

He reached for a plate then figured, why dirty another dish, and set the whole thing in the microwave.

While he waited for it to heat, he noticed his wallet lying on the counter and out of habit slipped it into his pants pocket. He wasn't worried about the cash so much as his credit and ATM cards. The last time Ian had stayed with their brother Victor, he'd run off with his Mastercard and charged several thousand pounds' worth of purchases before Vic even realized the card was missing. Electronic equipment mostly, which Garrett figured Ian had probably sold for cash.

Garrett wasn't taking any chances. After a shower and a meal and a good night's sleep, he would loan Ian a few hundred pounds—that he knew would never be repaid—and send him on his merry way. With any luck, he wouldn't darken Garrett's doorway again for a very long time.

Ian emerged a few minutes later, freshly shaven, his hair still damp, wearing rumpled but clean clothes. "Best shower I ever had," he told Garrett.

"I made you tea."

He saw the cup and scowled. "I don't suppose you have anything stronger."

Garrett shrugged and said, "Sorry." Unless he wanted

his liquor cabinet cleaned out, Garrett was keeping it securely locked for the duration of his brother's visit. Besides, Ian probably had a bottle or two stashed in his duffel. Given the choice between a meal and a bottle of cheap whiskey, the alcohol always won.

"Well, then, tea it is," Ian conceded, as though he had a choice. "You just get in from work?"

"Why do you ask?"

"Came by earlier, but you weren't here. I waited for you in the park across the road."

It was a wonder he wasn't arrested for loitering. The authorities in this neighborhood had no tolerance for riffraff. "I wasn't working."

"Got a lady friend then, do you? Anyone I know?"

Garrett nearly chuckled at the thought of Ian socializing with the royal family. "No one you know."

The microwave beeped and Garrett pulled out the dish.

Knowing Garrett couldn't cook worth a damn, Ian eyed the food suspiciously. "You made that?"

"Don't worry, my housekeeper prepared it."

"In that case, slide it this way," Ian said, rubbing his work-roughened hands together in anticipation. Garrett watched as he shoveled a forkful into his mouth, eating right there at the kitchen counter, standing up.

"Delicious," he mumbled through a mouthful of beef and potatoes. He followed it with a swallow of tea. He wolfed down the food with an embarrassing lack of regard for the most basic table manners. Their mum would have been horrified. They may have lived like paupers but his mum had always insisted they carry themselves with dignity.

"So," Garrett asked, "why did you get fired this time?"

"Who says I was fired?" Ian asked indignantly.

"Please don't insult my intelligence."

He relented and answered, "The owner of the ranch caught me in the hay barn with his youngest daughter."

"How young?"

"Seventeen."

Garrett was about to say that a twenty-eight-year-old man had no business chasing a girl more than ten years his junior, but that was almost exactly the age difference between himself and Louisa. But that was different. Louisa was an adult—even if her family didn't treat her like one. Not to mention that Garrett intended to marry her, while he was quite sure his brother was only using the young girl in question.

"Don't give me that look of disapproval," Ian countered. "It wasn't my fault. She seduced me."

Of course. Nothing was ever his fault. Someone else was always to blame for his irresponsibility. "Did you ever consider telling her no?"

"If you'd seen her, you wouldn't have told her no, either."

Unlike his brother, Garrett wasn't a slave to his hormones. He had principles. He didn't take advantage of women. Not sexually, anyway. Besides, he wasn't taking advantage of Louisa. If she married him, she would never be denied a thing she desired. With the exception of a few children, that is.

"What are you going to do now?" he asked Ian.

"Like I said, I have something fantastic in the works.

A sure thing. I just need a bit of capital to get it off the ground."

He didn't say it, but Garrett knew exactly what he was thinking and saved him the trouble of having to ask. "Don't look at me. I've thrown away enough money on your so-called sure things."

Ian shrugged. "Your loss."

Garrett doubted that.

Ian finished his dinner, stopping just shy of licking the dish clean. "Delicious. Best meal I've had in weeks."

"I assume you need a place to stay."

He leaned back against the countertop and folded his arms over his chest. "There's a very comfortable bench in the park I could sleep on."

"You're welcome to use the spare bedroom. For *one* night," he stressed. "And I expect everything to be as you found it when you go."

"I'll even make the bed."

"Well then, I'm off to bed," Garrett said.

"Already? I thought we might catch up for a while."

"I have an early breakfast meeting."

Ian looked appalled. "You're working on a Saturday?"

"Sometimes I work Sundays, as well." A concept Ian, who worked as little as possible, would never grasp. "Help yourself to whatever you find in the icebox, and I have satellite television if you want to watch it. I'll see you in the morning."

"See you in the morning," Ian parroted as Garrett walked from the room. He felt uncomfortable leaving his brother to his own devices, but short of staying awake all night, he didn't have much choice.

Consequently, Garrett didn't see Ian in the morning.

When he rolled out of bed at 6:00 a.m., Ian had already left. With half the contents of the liquor cabinet and Garrett's car.

The e-mail showed up in Louisa's personal in-box late Saturday afternoon. At first when she saw the blank subject line she assumed it was junk mail, then she noticed the return address—G.B. Man—and her heart nearly stopped.

That couldn't be a coincidence. It had to be him.

Not now, she thought to herself. Not when things were going so well. She took a deep breath, preparing herself for the worst, and reluctantly double clicked to open it. The body of the e-mail read simply, Did you miss me, Princess?

No gruesome nursery rhymes or threats of violence this time, still a cold chill slithered up her spine. This was going to put everyone into a panic and security back on high alert. Which meant her chances of leaving the castle and going on a normal date with Garrett were slim to none. Why did the Gingerbread Man have to choose now to start harassing them again?

She leaned over for the phone to ring security, when she noticed the time stamp on the e-mail and realized it had actually been sent yesterday morning. Louisa didn't check her in-box daily, but her brothers did. If they had gotten one, too, wouldn't she have heard about it by now?

Was it possible that the Gingerbread Man had sent a message to her alone? And if so, was it a coincidence that it started at the same time she began seeing Garrett? Was he trying to complicate things?

She sat back in her chair, wondering what she should

do. The e-mail hadn't been threatening at all. Just a reminder that he was still there, which they all had assumed anyway. If he had planned to actually harm a member of the family, wouldn't he have done it by now?

If she accidentally forgot to mention this to security, what difference would it really make?

She sat there with her finger hovering over the delete button, weighing her options. If it turned out her brothers and sister had gotten an e-mail, too, she could just tell them that she must have erased hers accidentally, assuming it was junk mail. She hated to lie, but this was her future on the line. Her relationship with Garrett might be destiny, but even destiny had its limits. Would Garrett want to court a woman who wasn't even allowed to leave the house, and by dating her very possibly make *himself* a target?

It would be best, for now, if no one else knew about this.

Before she could change her mind, she stabbed the delete key, promising herself that if he contacted her again, threatening or not, she would let the family know. Until then, it would be her secret.

Six

It was after noon when Garrett's meeting finally ended. He was in the company limo on his way to the club to play squash with Wes, when he received a call from the police informing him that his car had been in an accident. Apparently, in his haste to flee Garrett's town house, Ian had run off the road and into a tree.

"He was pretty banged up," the officer told him. "But he was conscious and alert when they put him in the ambulance."

Despite everything, Garrett was relieved Ian wasn't hurt too badly. If he'd died, Garrett would have been the one to break the news to his family. Since it was Garrett's car Ian had been driving, they would likely pin the blame on him. Not that he cared what they thought of him any longer. It was just a hassle he didn't need.

"Did he say how it happened?" Garrett asked.

"He claims he swerved to avoid hitting an animal in the road, a dog, and lost control."

Ian had always had a soft spot for animals. Dogs especially, so it was a plausible excuse.

Garrett dreaded the next question he had to ask. "Was alcohol involved?"

"We assumed so at first. There were a dozen or so broken bottles of liquor in the car. Expensive stuff, too."

Tell me about it, Garrett wanted to say.

"He denied being intoxicated, but we won't know for certain until we get the results of the blood test. He must have been going quite fast though. I'm sorry to say that the car is totaled."

It wouldn't be the first car Ian had demolished with his careless driving. Or the last. Besides, Garrett had never expected to get it back. He didn't have the heart to report it as stolen and Ian would have eventually sold it. At least now Garrett would get the insurance money, and Ian would have to face what he'd done while the wounds were still fresh.

He thanked the officer for the information and instructed his driver to take him to the hospital instead, then rang Wes to cancel. With any luck, this fiasco wouldn't find its way into the papers, or, if it did, he hoped no names were released. With the royal family keeping a close eye on him, the last thing he needed was a scandal. Not that he should be held accountable for his brother's actions, but in his experience royals had a... *unique* way of looking at things.

Garrett should have listened to his instincts and never let Ian in the house. Or maybe this time Ian would finally learn his lesson.

The limo dropped him at the front entrance of the hospital and Garrett stopped at the information desk to get his brother's room number. Ian's was on the third floor just past the nursing station, but when Garrett walked through the door, he was totally unprepared for what he saw. He'd expected Ian to have suffered a few bumps and bruises, maybe a laceration or two, but his baby brother looked as though he'd gone a dozen rounds with a prize fighter.

His face was swollen and bruised, his nose broken and both eyes blackened. His right wrist and hand were wrapped in gauze, and he'd suffered small nicks and cuts on both arms. From the broken bottles, Garrett figured. His left leg was in a cast from foot to midthigh and suspended in a sling.

Garrett shook his head and thought, *Ian, what have you done to yourself?*

Instead of seeing Ian the troublemaker lying there, under the bandages and bruises Garrett could only picture the little boy who used to come to him with skinned knees and splinters, and his anger swiftly fizzled away.

"Garrett Sutherland?" someone asked from behind him.

He turned to find a doctor standing just outside the room. "Yes."

"Dr. Sacsner," he said, shaking Garrett's hand. "I'm your brother's surgeon."

"Surgeon?"

"Orthopedics." He gestured out of the room. "Could we have a word?"

Garrett nodded and followed him into the hallway.

"Your brother is a lucky man," the doctor began to say.

"He doesn't look so lucky to me."

"I know it looks bad, but it could have been much worse. The fact that he suffered no internal injuries is nothing short of a miracle."

"What about his leg?"

The doctor frowned. "There he wasn't so lucky. His lower leg was crushed under the dash. The impact shattered the fibula and snapped his tibia in three places. The only thing holding it together are rods and pins."

"But he'll recover?"

"With time and physical therapy he should make a full recovery. The first six weeks will be the most difficult. It's imperative he stay off the leg as much as possible and keep it elevated."

"So he'll stay here?"

"For another day or two, then he'll be released."

Released? Where was he going to go?

He realized, by the doctor's expression, that Garrett was expected to take Ian home.

Bloody hell. He didn't have time for this now. Nor did he feel he owed his brother a thing after all the grief he'd caused. But who else did Ian have? Where else could he stay?

"I know it sounds like a daunting task," the doctor said. "But if money is no object, you can hire twenty-four-hour care if necessary." His pager beeped and he checked the display. "I'll be back to check on him later."

"Before you go, was it determined if alcohol was involved?"

"That was a concern at first, since he came in smelling

like a distillery. We were hesitant to give him anything for the pain, but he swore he wasn't drinking, and the tox screen came back clean. No drugs or alcohol in his system."

So he had just been driving too fast and lost control. If that wasn't Ian's life story. As a kid he was always pushing the limits and hurting himself. If there was a tree too high or dangerous to climb, Ian wasn't happy until he reached the highest branch. By the time he was eight, he'd suffered more broken bones and received more stitches than most people did in a lifetime.

Maybe this time he would learn his lesson.

"You didn't have to come here," he heard his brother say, his voice rusty from the anesthesia.

Garrett turned and walked to his bed. "Someone has to pay the bill."

Ian gazed up at him, bleary-eyed and fuzzy. "I guess 'I'm sorry' isn't going to cut it this time."

"It might if I thought you meant it." But Ian wasn't sorry for all the trouble he'd caused. Only that he'd been caught.

His eyes drifted shut, and Garrett thought that maybe he'd fallen asleep, then he opened them again and said, "I was going to bring it back."

"The car or the liquor?"

"Both."

Garrett wished he could believe that.

"I got a few miles from your house and I started to feel guilty."

That was even more unbelievable. "You don't do guilt."

"Apparently I do now. I thought if I got back fast

enough you would never know I'd left. Then that damned dog darted out in front of me." Ian studied him for several seconds. "You don't believe me."

"Is there a reason I should?"

He sighed. "Well, whether you believe me or not, I'm tired of living this way. I'm going to change this time. I swear I am."

Garrett might have believed his brother if he hadn't heard the same thing so many times before. "Let's just concentrate on getting you healthy. The doctor says you have to keep off the leg for six weeks. With my hectic schedule, I'll have to hire a nurse to stay with you."

"You don't have to do that."

And he didn't expect a penny of it back. "Where else would you go? You think Mum and Dad would let you stay with them?"

His expression said he knew the answer to that question was no. Even if their mother still had a soft spot for Ian, their father would put his foot down.

"I'll figure something out," Ian declared.

"You have a friend who will take you in?"

Ian was silent. They both knew that Ian had never made a friend he didn't eventually betray. Unfortunately, Garrett was all he had. "You're staying with me."

"I owe you too much already," Ian said, and Garrett wished the regret he heard in his brother's voice was genuine. He wasn't counting on it though.

"Face it, Ian, we're stuck with each other. If you really mean what you say about turning over a new leaf—"

"I do. I swear it."

"Then you can spend the next six weeks proving it to me."

* * *

Louisa woke early Sunday morning, planning her picnic with Garrett before she even got out of bed, until she heard the low rumble of thunder and the thrum of rain against her bedroom window.

Oh, damn!

Rubbing the sleep from her eyes, she climbed out of bed, rousing Muffin, who gave a grumble of irritation before settling back to sleep. She walked to the window and shoved the curtains aside. Dense gray clouds rolled in from the northwest, and a fierce wind pummeled the trees and whipped rain against the windows.

She sighed. It looked as though the weather front that was supposed to miss the island had changed course sometime during the night. It was only 7:00 a.m., but even if the rain stopped it would still be too wet for a picnic. She'd been so sure it would be a sunny day, she hadn't bothered with a plan B. Her options were limited considering she couldn't leave the castle with Garrett without giving Chris a two-day warning. And with the weather so dreary, she doubted that he and Melissa would be doing any sailing today.

So much for her and Garrett having some time to themselves. If they had to stay inside the castle, someone would be constantly looking over their shoulders, watching their every move.

She frowned. Being royalty, especially royalty under house arrest, could be terribly inconvenient.

But she refused to let this small setback dampen her spirits. She was sure if she put her mind to it, she could come up with something for them to do, some indoor activity they would both enjoy. Maybe a tour of the castle or a game of billiards. Or maybe they could just sit and talk.

On her way to the shower, Louisa passed her computer and was half tempted to log on, just to see if she had gotten another e-mail from their stalker. No one had said anything about getting the e-mail yesterday, so she could only assume his latest communication had been sent exclusively to her. She couldn't help wondering if her relationship with Garrett was the catalyst or if it was just a coincidence that he chose now to pick on her individually.

Maybe she should check, just in case. She took a step toward her computer, then stopped. What would be the point of checking? If he e-mailed her, he e-mailed her and nothing would change that, and the way she looked at it, what she didn't know wouldn't hurt her.

She gave her computer one last furtive glance and headed to the bathroom instead.

She showered using her favorite rose-scented body wash and took extra care fixing her hair. Instead of the conservative bun she typically wore, she used hot rollers then brushed her hair smooth, until it lay loose and silky down her back. She dressed in pale pink capris and a crème-colored cashmere sweater set, then slipped her feet into a pair of pink leather flats. She rounded out the look with mascara and pink, cherry-flavored lip gloss with a touch of glitter.

She stood back to examine her reflection, happy with what she saw, sure that Garrett would be pleased, too.

Anticipation adding an extra lift to her step, she headed downstairs to the dining room for a spot of tea, Muffin trailing behind her, but Geoffrey intercepted her at the foot of the stairs.

"Prince Christian asked that you call him as soon as possible."

She frowned. "Call him? Did they go sailing? The weather is horrible."

"No, Your Highness. He took Princess Melissa to the hospital early this morning."

Her heart skipped a beat. "What for?"

"He didn't say. He just asked that you call him as soon as you're up."

"Are Aaron and Liv up yet?"

"Not yet."

She was going to ask him to wake them, but there was no sense in starting a panic before she even knew what was wrong. It might be nothing.

"Could you see that Muffin is fed and let out?" she asked Geoffrey.

"Of course. Come along, Muffin."

Muffin just stood there looking back and forth between them.

"Breakfast," Geoffrey added, and Muffin scurried excitedly after him.

Forgetting about her tea, Louisa hurried back to her room and dialed her brother's cell phone. As soon as he answered she asked, "What's wrong? Is Melissa okay? Are the babies all right?"

Chris chuckled and said, "Relax, everyone is fine. Melissa started having contractions last night."

"Why didn't you wake me?"

"There was nothing you could have done and Melissa didn't want you to worry."

"Is she in labor? I thought it was too early."

"She was, but they gave her a drug to stop it. Unfortunately she's already dilated two centimeters, so she's on complete bed rest. They're keeping her in the hospital until she delivers."

"Oh, Chris, I'm so sorry. Is there anything I can do?"

"Actually, yes. Melissa made a list of things she needs. Makeup and toiletries and things like that. Could you gather everything and bring it to the hospital?"

"Of course." She grabbed a pad of paper and a pen and jotted down the list. "I'll be there as soon as I can."

"I want to stay here as often as possible, so I'd like you to meet with my assistant about taking my place at a few speeches and charity events."

For a second she was struck dumb. He never would have trusted her to a task like that before. She almost asked, what about Aaron or Anne, but caught herself at the last minute. She didn't want him to think she didn't want to do it.

"Of course I will," she told him instead. "Anything."

"Thanks, Louisa. I'll see you soon."

She hung up and was turning to leave her room when she remembered her date with Garrett and stopped dead in her tracks.

Bloody hell.

Well, as much as she wanted to see Garrett, family always came first. Especially now, when Chris seemed to be seeing her as a capable adult. She would just have to call him and reschedule. Maybe they could see each other later in the week.

She picked up the phone, mumbling to herself about bad timing, but as she put it to her ear there was no dial tone. She nearly jumped out of her skin when a deep male voice said, "Hello?"

"Garrett?"

"Well, that was strange," he said.

"What just happened?"

"I called your number, but before it could even ring, I heard your voice."

"Seriously? Because I just picked up the phone so I could call you!"

Garrett chuckled. "We must be on the same brain wave or something."

"I guess. Why were you calling?"

"Regrettably, something came up and I have to break our date for this afternoon."

Louisa laughed and said, "Seriously?"

Garrett paused for several seconds, then said, "Well, that wasn't exactly the reaction I'd been expecting."

"I'm laughing because I was calling you to say that *I* have to cancel our date."

"Hmm, that is pretty weird, isn't it?"

"I thought maybe we could get together later this week."

"We could do that. The first half of the week will be a little hectic for me, but maybe Thursday evening?"

That seemed so far off, but at least it would give her time to visit with Melissa while she adjusted to being confined to a hospital bed. "Just to warn you, if you want to take me off the palace grounds, Chris will need two days' warning to arrange for security."

"Well, then, I guess I'll call you Tuesday." There was a commotion in the background, and what sounded like a voice over a PA system, but she couldn't make out what they were saying. "I'm sorry, Louisa, but I have to go. I'll talk to you Tuesday."

Before she could say goodbye, he disconnected, and

she realized she hadn't even asked why he had to cancel today. Oh well, she was sure that it must have been very important. They could talk about it Tuesday.

She hated the thought of having to wait until Thursday to see Garrett again, but the anticipation would make their next date that much more special.

Seven

Sunday morning became a blur of doctors and nurses and representatives from the private home care facility that Garrett was hiring to look after his brother while his leg healed. And since Ian was being released tomorrow morning, there wasn't much time to get everything squared away.

Though Garrett wasn't too keen on the idea of his brother staying in his house for another six weeks or so, at least this time Ian would be physically incapable of running off with his belongings. The only time he was allowed out of bed was to bathe and use the loo, or he risked the bones shifting and healing incorrectly, leaving him with the threat of more surgeries and possible permanent disabilities. And while Ian could be irresponsible and self-absorbed, he wasn't stupid.

It was going on three when all the arrangements were completed and the appropriate paperwork signed. Garrett was walking down the hall to the elevator when someone called his name. He turned to see Louisa standing behind him, flanked by two very large and ominous looking bodyguards.

Oddly enough, his first instinct was to pull her close and kiss her, and he might have were it not for the risk of being tackled by her security detail.

"I thought that was you," she said, breaking into a wide smile. "What are you doing here? Did you come to see Melissa?"

"Melissa?" he asked.

She walked toward him, and with a subtle wave of her hand the guards fell back several steps. "Princess Melissa, my sister-in-law."

"No. Is she here?"

"In the family's private wing," she said, gesturing behind her. "She was brought in last night for early labor. That's why I had to postpone our date."

"I had no idea. I'm here visiting...an associate. He was in an accident yesterday."

"Oh, I'm so sorry. Is he okay?"

"He's banged up, but he'll recover."

"Is that why you had to break our date? To come here?"

He nodded. "Weird, huh?"

"Very weird. If we knew we were both coming here we could have carpooled," she joked.

He grinned. "Except I was already here when I called you."

"He must be a special friend for you to stay here all day with him."

"We've known each other most of our lives." He knew he should probably tell her the truth, but he just didn't feel like explaining. With any luck Ian would heal, then be out of Garrett's life forever, and the royal family would never be the wiser. "Is Melissa all right?"

"They managed to stop her labor, but she's on strict bed rest for at least four weeks, and they're keeping her in the hospital just to be safe."

"Please send her and Chris my best."

"She's having some tests right now, but I'm sure she would love a visit from you later. She's only been here a few hours and already she's crawling out of her skin."

Normally he wouldn't visit a stranger, but under the circumstances, it couldn't hurt. Besides, he'd liked Melissa from the moment he met her. She wasn't a typical royal. Of course neither was Liv, or Louisa for that matter. Maybe there was nothing unusual about any of them. Maybe it was his preconceived notion that was way off.

"I'd like that," he said. "As long as it's not an imposition."

"Of course not. Chris and Melissa really like you. In fact, Chris told me…" She paused and pressed her fingers to her lips.

"Chris told you what?"

Her cheeks flushed to match the pink of her pants. "Forget it."

He smiled. "You're blushing, Your Highness."

"I'm not sure if I should have said anything."

He folded his arms over his chest. She was usually so poised and self-confident. He liked that she had a vulnerable side. "Maybe you shouldn't have, but now you've piqued my curiosity. It wouldn't be fair to leave me hanging with no explanation, would it?"

"I suppose not." She glanced over at the busy nurses' station, then whispered, "Not here."

Whatever she had to say, it was apparently private in nature. All the more reason for him to know what was said. "Where?"

"I was on my way back to our private waiting room," she told him. "You could join me."

"I'd like that," he told her, realizing it was true, and not just for the information. Meeting like this in the hospital hallway could have been awkward, but instead he felt totally at ease with her. In fact, the moment he saw her standing there, some of the stress from the last few days seemed to melt away.

He held out his arm and she slipped hers through it. Thankfully the guards didn't knock him to the ground and cuff him. "Lead the way, Your Highness."

Louisa led Garrett into the royal family's private waiting room. She was relieved to find it empty. If this was the only time they could be alone, she could think of worse places.

"This is nice," Garrett said, gazing around. "More like a hotel suite than a hospital."

"It didn't used to be so modern, but the last few years, with my father's condition, we've spent a lot of time here so it was renovated."

"I expected Chris to be here."

"He's with Melissa. She's having a test to determine the development of the babies' lungs." She turned to set down her purse and felt Garrett's hands settle on her shoulders. A warm and delicious feeling poured through her like honey and the purse dropped with a clunk on the table.

"Does that mean we're alone?" he asked, and something in his tone made her heart skip a beat. Until now, she was the one to instigate the physical contact. It was exciting, and yes, maybe a little scary, that he had taken the upper hand.

"I guess we are."

His hands slipped off her shoulders and down her arms. His palms were smooth and felt hot to the touch. "Security won't barge in at any second?"

"Only if I call them."

"Are you going to call them?"

Now that they *finally* had some time alone? *Not bloody likely.* "I wasn't planning on it."

"Even if I do this?" He pulled her hair over one shoulder and brushed a kiss on the back of her neck. Goose bumps broke out across her skin, and her legs suddenly felt limp. Men had kissed her before, but it had been a long time since one made her tingle all over or feel the warm tug of arousal between her thighs and in her breasts.

He kissed her shoulder and she willed him to touch her, to cup her breasts in his palms, to slide his hand down, inside her panties. She almost moaned out loud imagining it, but she knew this wasn't the time or the place.

"I like your hair this way," he said, running his fingers through it. "You should wear it down all the time."

"Maybe I will."

"You were going to tell me what Chris said," he reminded her, his breath warm on her nape where he dropped soft kisses.

"I'd hoped you'd forgotten about that." She let her head fall to the side, giving him more area to explore, and he didn't disappoint. "Chris might be upset that I told you."

"We'll keep it between you and me."

"You promise?"

He turned her to face him and brushed his lips across hers. "Cross my heart and hope to die."

Even if she'd wanted to tell him no, there was no way she could. He could ask her the royal family's most intimate secrets right now and they would spill willingly from the lips he so skillfully nibbled. "I was talking to Chris the other day and he mentioned that if…well, if you and I were to get married, you would be a good choice to replace Aaron when he goes back to school."

He stopped kissing her. "He said that?"

"Just the other day."

"Well, I'm…I'm a bit speechless, actually. I'm flattered that he would even consider me."

"Nothing is set in stone, of course, which is why I never should have said anything in the first place. Me and my big mouth."

He smiled and made a growling sound deep in his throat. He cradled her face in his hand and brushed the pad of his thumb across her lower lip. "Hmm, I love your mouth."

She loved the way it felt when he touched it. Especially when he used his lips.

"Chris also insinuated that we shouldn't 'rush' things," she said.

"Are we rushing?"

She grinned up at him. "As far as I'm concerned, we're not moving fast enough. In fact, would you find it totally inappropriate to make out on the sofa in a hospital waiting room?"

"If it were only kissing, maybe not, but I'm having a tough time keeping my hands off of you."

She sighed and laid her head against his chest, heard the steady thump of his heart. "There has to be someplace we can go to be completely alone."

"I have a place in Cabo," he offered. "Maybe with enough advance warning, your family would let you go."

"I would *love* that! I'll talk to Chris about it."

"Unless security issues aren't his only concern."

She didn't have to ask what he meant. "I'm twenty-seven. My sex life is none of my family's business. And believe me when I say that they're in no position whatsoever to pass judgment. I hate that we have to even talk about this, that we can't just be a normal couple, let things happen naturally."

He led her to the sofa, pulling her close beside him as they sat. "All couples have issues, Louisa."

She drew her legs up over his thighs and curled against his chest. "Sometimes I wish I could lead a normal life. I'd like to shop in a store without a team of security parked outside, or eat dinner in a restaurant without a thorough background check of every employee." She looked up at him. "Have you ever considered what it would be like to be in a relationship with someone like me? The freedoms you would have to sacrifice? You'd be a fool not to run screaming in the opposite direction."

"Those things don't matter to me, Louisa." He cradled her chin in his hand and gazed into her eyes. They were so dark and compassionate and earnest it made her want to cry. "The way I feel about you, I'd be a fool not to stay."

He brushed his lips against hers, so tenderly. So sweet. But she didn't want tender and sweet. She was tired of that. She wanted fire and passion. She wanted to feel sexy and desired.

She slid her hands around Garrett's neck, pulled him down and kissed him. A kiss that was anything but tender. At first he resisted a little, until she drew herself up on her knees and straddled his lap.

"I can't seem to control myself when I'm with you," he mumbled against her lips.

"Good, because neither can I." She rocked her hips and rubbed against him. Garrett growled deep in his throat and tunneled his fingers through her hair, feeding off her mouth. She could feel his erection growing between them and she wanted so badly to touch him. She was so far gone, she didn't care that Chris could walk through the door at any second.

Which incidentally, he did.

Somewhere in the back of her hormone-drenched brain she heard the door open, then the exaggerated rumble of a throat clearing. She peeled herself away from Garrett and looked over to find Chris in the waiting room doorway, one brow lifted. She knew exactly what he was thinking. This was her idea of discretion?

She heard Garrett mumble a particularly colorful curse under his breath—one most men wouldn't dare speak in front of a princess—as he lifted her from his lap and dropped her onto the sofa beside him.

"Sorry to interrupt," Chris said, "but Melissa is back in her room and eager for visitors."

Louisa should have asked how Melissa was doing, or if the babies were okay, but to her surprise, and apparently her brother's surprise as well, the first thing out of her mouth was, "I'm going to Cabo with Garrett and you can't stop me."

Demanding she be allowed to leave the country with Garrett probably hadn't been the wisest course of action for Louisa to win a little freedom. Especially when Chris had just walked in on them making out like two lust-driven youths. Garrett was quite sure, considering her brother's look of exasperation, she wouldn't be leaving the country anytime soon. With Garrett or anyone else.

So much for convincing her family that he wasn't compromising her honor.

Garrett assumed Chris would be furious with him, but when he pulled the Prince aside later to apologize for his inappropriate behavior, Chris only laughed.

"I know you're smarter than that, Garrett. I don't believe for a second that my sister wasn't the aggressor. Just, if you could, try to keep her in check, at least when you're in public. I would appreciate it."

Garrett had been so stunned, he couldn't form a coherent reply, which seemed to amuse Chris even more.

"You think I don't know what my sister is like?"

"She can be…tenacious," Garrett said.

Chris chuckled. "That's putting it mildly. I've spent the better part of my life keeping her out of trouble. She whines incessantly that we shelter her, yet she refuses to exercise any common sense. If she wants something she goes after it, all pistons firing. Usually with no regard to the rules, or oftentimes her own safety. And if what she gets isn't what she wanted, watch out.

"Don't get me wrong, I love my sister to death. She has a heart of gold and you'll never meet a woman more loyal to her family and friends. I would lay down my life for her. I also believe that she'll make a fantastic wife and mother. But she is a handful. Let your guard down and she'll walk all over you."

In other words, her so-called reputation of being sweet and naive was *bollocks*. He'd basically figured that out already. He just hadn't realized the extent of her defiance. Some men might have considered that a negative quality, and maybe he should have, too, but the idea that she wasn't at all what he expected only intrigued him more.

The question was: what did Chris have to gain by his honesty? Was he trying to scare Garrett away? And why would he after he'd told Louisa that he was considering offering Aaron's position to Garrett?

"Why are you telling me this?" he asked Chris.

"I think you should know what you're getting yourself into. Louisa needs a man who's just as headstrong and determined as she is, and I see those qualities in you. She needs someone who can…rein her in."

He made it sound as though Louisa needed a babysitter more than a husband. Did the royal family cling to the archaic values that deemed women should be seen but not heard?

He wasn't sure if he should feel grateful for Chris's candid advice, or offended on Louisa's behalf. And since when did Garrett feel the need to defend her? When did he start caring about her feelings?

Probably right around the same time she smiled up at him and said she couldn't wait to see him naked.

"By the way," Chris said. "Send me a copy of your itinerary and I'll see what I can do. It will take at least two weeks to arrange."

It took a second for Garett to realize he was talking about the trip to Cabo. "I assumed that wasn't going to happen."

"If I tell her no, there's a good chance she'll go without permission. Besides, maybe some time away would do her good. With our father in fairly stable condition, I think we could all use a vacation."

Garrett, too, was looking forward to some time away. With his brother around, the less time he spent at home, the better as far as he was concerned. He and Ian had nothing left to say to one another, and all that talk about Ian changing his ways was rubbish. Ian would never change.

After a short visit with Melissa, who was indeed climbing the walls, Garrett said goodbye to Louisa, sealing their departure with another enthusiastic kiss. He made a short trip to the office to get a few documents that needed his attention. Then, because the cook had Sundays off, he picked up dinner on his way home.

Later, as he lounged in front of the television, mindlessly surfing the channels, he thought about calling Louisa to see if Melissa's tests came back favorable. Only, as usual, she called him first.

He picked up the phone after the first ring and said, "You probably won't believe this, but I was just about to call you."

"Were you really?" a sultry voice purred in his ear. "And here I thought you'd forgotten all about me."

The unfamiliar voice threw him for a moment, then he looked at the caller ID and realized it wasn't Louisa after all. It was Pamela, a woman he dated on occasion. Although to call what they did "dating" was a gross overstatement. They had sex. Unemotional, uncomplicated, no-strings-attached sex. Just the way he liked it.

"Pamela, sorry, I thought you were someone else," he said. "How have you been?"

Her voice dripped with the promise of something naughty. "Missing you terribly, love."

He used to find her sultry drawl warm and sexy. Now he recognized it for what it was: as insincere as her affection for him. She was using him, just as he had used her. Up until today that hadn't bothered him in the least, in fact he'd preferred it that way, but now it just seemed…sleazy.

"I've been busy," he said, but she totally missed what he'd hoped was a direct brush-off.

"Well, if you're not busy tonight, why don't I stop by for a while? We could get…reacquainted."

It wasn't the only time she'd offered herself up freely to him, but for the first time, he wasn't the least bit interested. Not that he had no appetite for female companionship, but the female he was interested in right now was Louisa.

"I'm afraid this isn't a good time," he told Pamela.

"How about tomorrow night instead?"

"That won't be a good time, either."

The sexy tone wavered, as though she was finally starting to catch on that something was up. "When *would* it be a good time?"

How about never? "The thing is, Pamela, I'm seeing someone."

"So?"

Admittedly, in the past, that wouldn't have stopped him. "What I mean is, I'm seeing someone...*special.*"

There was a pause, then a short burst of laughter. "Are you saying that you're in a serious relationship?"

"I am," he said, relieved that he didn't have to spell it out. Sometimes he could hardly believe it himself.

"Is she pregnant?"

"No, she's not pregnant."

"Blackmailing you?"

He laughed. "Is it so hard to believe I met a woman I want to date seriously?"

"I've known you almost ten years, Garrett, and in all that time not once did you ever have a serious relationship. You're far too selfish."

Pamela was right, but that selfish streak had led him to where he was now. He didn't miss the irony. Some might go so far as saying he was too selfish for his own good.

"Who's the lucky girl? Anyone I know?"

"No one you know," he assured her. Of course she knew *of* Louisa, but they had certainly never inhabited the same social circles.

"Well, I guess all I can say is good luck," Pamela said.

He said his goodbyes, hung up, then permanently deleted her number from his phone. He was about to set it down on the table beside him when it rang again.

This time it was Louisa, and he caught himself smiling. "I was just thinking about calling you," he said.

"Were you?" There was a distinct note of happiness in her voice.

"I wondered if you'd heard the results from Melissa's tests." As soon as the words left his mouth, he knew they were not entirely true. If he had called, it would have been just to talk to her. To hear her voice.

"How sweet of you," she responded, buying his fib without question. "She got the results just a bit ago and unfortunately the babies' lungs need at least a few more weeks to develop. They've started her on steroids to get things moving along. On the bright side, she hasn't had any more contractions."

"That's good news."

"Do you know why I called you?" she asked.

"Why?"

"I was lying in bed thinking about our kiss today and I just wanted to hear your voice."

Eight

Garrett found himself envying Louisa's unrelenting honesty. Why was he so incapable of expressing his feelings? Or maybe in her case, his discretion was the kindest thing he had to offer. Was it fair to lead her on when the emotions he was feeling now were driven by curiosity and fleeting at best?

He didn't think so.

"I'm starting to feel like I'll go crazy if we don't get some time alone soon," she said.

He could relate. If Chris hadn't stepped in the room when he did, things might have gotten out of hand. "I know what you mean."

"I think about it a lot," she admitted.

"Think about what?"

"Sex."

He sat up a little straighter in his chair. "You do?"

"I fantasize *all* the time."

"About what?"

"You. What it will be like when we're finally alone. How you'll touch me, and what it will feel like to touch you. Sometimes I get myself so worked up thinking about it that I have to…well, you know."

She couldn't possibly be saying what he thought she was saying. "You have to what?"

"*Touch* myself."

Bloody hell. He formed a mental picture of that and just about swallowed his tongue.

"I've been doing a lot of reading on the Internet, too," she said.

"What kind of reading?"

"Erotic short stories mostly. My favorites are the romantic ones, but there are a few with a bondage theme I thought were kind of fun."

Bloody hell. Now would be an excellent time to change the subject, but his brain just wasn't cooperating. Probably because all the blood in his body was pooling in the vicinity of his crotch. He was so hard he had to unfasten the button fly on his jeans.

"Nothing too extreme, of course. But I think I'd be willing to try silk scarves and feathers."

He resisted the visual representation, but it popped into his head anyway.

He was so stiff he was aching, and he was seriously considering asking what her feelings were on phone sex, but if he and Louisa were going to be intimate, he'd be damned if he was going to do it from across town.

"Are you trying to drive me insane?" he asked, and she laughed.

"Maybe. Is it working?"

"I'm in agony."

"You wouldn't believe all of the different things I could do to help you with that."

And, of course, a dozen or so instantly came to mind. "If you say another word, I swear to God I'm hanging up."

She laughed. "Okay, I promise I'll stop."

"All those rumors I've heard that you're inexperienced and pure—I'm not buying it."

"I hate to disappoint you, but the rumors are true."

"How is that even possible?"

"I was very sheltered. I wasn't even allowed to start dating until I was eighteen and when I did there was always a chaperone. I never had the chance to experiment, although not for lack of trying. Unfortunately, the more I tried, the tighter my family pulled back on the reins. It was as if everyone was determined to keep me unspoiled and pure. Eventually I got tired of fighting them and I just sort of, I don't know…lost interest, I guess."

"You seem interested now," he said.

"It was the Internet. I stumbled across a site full of stories and it opened up a whole new world to me. I finally started to realize what I've been missing all this time. It all just seemed so natural and…beautiful. I wanted to try everything. Well," she amended, "*almost* everything. When it comes to sex, people do some weird things."

"For the record, I'm not into weird."

"I'm glad," she said, sounding a little relieved.

"If you're so…interested, why don't you date more?"

"Because most men I meet are more interested in my wealth or my title than me."

How would she feel if she knew he was one of those men? That would remain his and Wes's secret.

"I find so many men, especially the ones close to my age, far too arrogant and entitled. So, here I am now, twenty-seven and still unspoiled, but dying to be corrupted. And don't ask me how, but when you took me in your arms on the dance floor, I just knew you were the one."

Though it made no sense at all, he felt honored that she had chosen him. "I can't say that I've ever corrupted anyone before, but I'd certainly be willing to give it a go. I'm free right now, in fact."

"Even with Chris and my parents gone, inviting you over at 11:30 p.m. might be pushing the envelope. But the time will come when we're completely alone, and I know it will be worth the wait. I just hope it's sooner rather than later."

"Me, too." What healthy heterosexual male didn't wish he had, at his disposal, a young, beautiful and sexy virgin willing to—in her own words—try practically everything? Men would pay exorbitant sums of money to trade places with him. And to think that he once believed he would have to take the sexual aspect of their courtship painfully slow. How completely wrong he'd been. This was working out far better than he ever could have imagined.

So why, somewhere deep down, did he feel so damned guilty?

The King had all the necessary adjustments performed on his heart pump Wednesday and the reinsertion after the capacity test went off without a hitch. Unfortunately, the news was not what they had hoped. Though some areas of the heart showed signs of healing, there had been little improvement in his overall heart function.

Everyone was disappointed, but Louisa refused to let the news get her down. As far as she was concerned, this was just a minor setback. His heart was just taking a little longer to heal, that's all.

Anne was still in England with their parents, so Louisa sat in a visitor's chair in Melissa's hospital room with Aaron, Liv, Chris, and of course Melissa, discussing how the setback would affect the family.

Chris sat on the edge of the bed with his wife. "Obviously I'll continue to perform Father's duties, and Aaron will cover my duties."

Liv leaned beside Aaron against the wall by the door. "But who will take over for Aaron when he starts school?" she asked, clearly concerned that his plans would be pushed aside yet another semester.

"I have a backup plan," Chris told her.

Aaron regarded him curiously. "Since when?"

"Recently," Chris said, glancing Louisa's way. "I'm considering offering a position to Garrett Sutherland."

Suddenly all eyes were on Louisa.

"What you mean is, if Louisa marries him," Melissa clarified.

Chris nodded. "Of course."

"He is more than qualified," Aaron confirmed.

"I agree," Melissa said. "But is it fair to put that kind of pressure on Louisa?"

"We're all under pressure," Chris told her. "Besides, she's always asking for more responsibility."

Louisa hated when they talked about her as though she wasn't sitting right there. Why did they insist on treating her like a child?

It was a moot point anyway. Their father was going to recover and resume his duties, then everything would go back to normal. These last couple years would be nothing more than a bad memory.

"What do *you* think, Louisa?" Liv asked.

Finally, she was part of the conversation. "I think you're blowing this way out of proportion. This is just a minor setback. Father will be fine."

She could tell by their expressions that they thought she was being naive, and she pitied them for their cynicism. This would be so much easier for all of them if they would just have faith.

No one scolded or tried to reason with her, and she was grateful for that, but she felt as though, if she didn't get out of there soon, she would lose her mind. Even though she wasn't supposed to see Garrett until tomorrow evening, that was one day too long as far as she was concerned.

She grabbed her purse and rose from her chair. "If the family discussion is over, I'm leaving."

"Where are you going?" Chris asked.

"Garrett is working from home today so I thought I would stop in and see him. If that's not a problem."

Chris and Aaron exchanged a look. Louisa honestly expected them to tell her no. In fact, she sort of hoped they would as she was itching for a fight. To her surprise though, Chris nodded and said, "Be sure to take a full detail with you. And you leave the vehicle only after the area has been secured."

"I know the rules," she snapped, and everyone looked surprised by her sharp tone. Did they think there was no limit to the flack she would take from them? That she was immune to their condescension?

"Remember that Anne is flying home and we're having dinner together here at the hospital," Chris told her, and there was an unspoken warning of *be there or else* in his tone. "Seven sharp."

If there was any way she could get out of it, she would, but for Melissa, who was desperate for company, Louisa couldn't say no. "I'll be here," she said and pulled the door open. Her bodyguards Gordon and Jack were waiting for her in the hall. She gestured to them and said, "We're leaving, gentlemen."

On the way to the car, Jack received a call on his cell. Chris, she was assuming, because when they got in the Bentley and she instructed Jack to take her to Garrett's town house he didn't bat an eyelash. It was a good thing she once again failed to mention the new e-mail she had gotten from the Gingerbread Man the day before. She would have mentioned it if there had been any direct threats or even an undertone of danger. All it had said was, Louisa and Garrett sitting in a tree K-I-S-S-I-N-G…

It was just his way of letting her know that he was keeping tabs on them. Par for the course.

When they got to Garrett's place, Louisa wasn't the least bit surprised to see that a team of security agents were already on the premises. Considering his net worth, she was a bit surprised he didn't live in a lavish home in a gated community. Not that his townhome wasn't very attractive, and very large, but he could afford much more. Although, she liked that he wasn't pretentious. Definitely not the kind of man interested in money and power.

It seemed to take forever before Gordon opened the car door and led her up the walk.

"You men will wait outside," she told him. Demanded

was more like it, even though she and Gordon both knew that he was obligated to do whatever Chris ordered. But he nodded and stepped to the side of the door where he had a clear view of the street. Louisa rang the bell, nearly buzzing with excitement at the idea of her and Garrett finally having some time to themselves.

It took him almost a full minute to answer the door, and when he did he was dressed more casually than she'd ever seen him, in lightweight jogging pants and a polo shirt with the emblem of the local yacht club embroidered over his left pec. The casual clothes for some reason seemed to accentuate his size. The thickness of his arms and the width of his shoulders. His lean waist and muscular thighs.

She expected a smile when he saw her standing there, maybe a hug and a kiss, but he just looked confused.

"Louisa? How did you...what are you doing here?"

It was true that Garrett hadn't technically invited her there, but she had been sure he wouldn't mind if she stopped by. How could he when they would get some much needed time alone? Wasn't that all they had been talking about? And why else would he mention, during their phone conversation Tuesday, that he would be working from home if he didn't want her to come over?

Now she wasn't so sure. Maybe the implied invitation hadn't been an invitation after all.

She pasted on a smile despite the sinking sensation in her belly. "I came to visit you."

"Chris let you?"

She nodded, keeping her smile bright. "I think he realized that if he forbid it, I might rebel." Garrett didn't

Send For
2 FREE BOOKS
Today!

I accept your offer!

Please send me two
free Silhouette Desire®
novels and two mystery
gifts (gifts worth about $10).
I understand that these books
are completely free—even
the shipping and handling will
be paid—and I am under no
obligation to purchase anything, ever,
as explained on the back of this card.

About how many NEW paperback fiction books have you purchased in the past 3 months?

❑ 0-2
E7WH

❑ 3-6
E7WT

❑ 7 or more
E7W5

225/326 SDL

Please Print

FIRST NAME

LAST NAME

ADDRESS

APT.#   CITY

STATE/PROV.   ZIP/POSTAL CODE

Visit us online at
www.ReaderService.com

S-D-07/10

▼ If offer card is missing write to: The Reader Service, P.O. Box 1867, Buffalo, NY 14240-1867 or visit www.ReaderService.com ▼

NO POSTAGE
NECESSARY
IF MAILED
IN THE
UNITED STATES

BUSINESS REPLY MAIL
FIRST-CLASS MAIL   PERMIT NO. 717   BUFFALO, NY

POSTAGE WILL BE PAID BY ADDRESSEE

THE READER SERVICE
PO BOX 1867
BUFFALO NY 14240-9952

say anything so she asked, "Aren't you going to invite me in?"

He looked behind him, into the town house, then back to her. "Um, sure, come on in."

He stepped aside to let her pass, but he was definitely edgy about something. He kept looking down a hallway that led to the rear of the unit. Behind him to the left was a staircase to the second floor.

She gazed around what was clearly a professionally decorated foyer and living room. It was undeniably male, but tastefully so. "This is nice."

He shrugged. "It suits my needs."

Why didn't he smile? Or take her into his arms and kiss her? Just a few nights ago he'd been dying to get his hands on her.

There was a brief, awkward silence, so she said brightly, "Aren't you going to offer me a tour?"

He shot another furtive glance behind him, and she began to wonder if he was with someone else. Maybe, despite his assurances that he was finished playing the field, he had another woman in his life. Her heart sank so hard and fast she could swear she felt it knocking around by her knees.

Please don't let him be like the others, she begged silently. He *had* to be the one. If not, her family would never let her live it down.

Garrett cleared his throat. "It's just that now isn't the best time."

Aware that her hands were shaking, she clasped them into fists, lifted her chin and asked him point blank, "Is there something you're not telling me?"

"Nothing that has anything to do with us. I promise. It's…complicated."

From down the hallway Louisa heard movement, then the timbre of a male voice called out, "Who is it, Garrett?"

It wasn't another woman, she thought with a relief that left her knees weak. Then it occurred to her, just because it was a man, it didn't mean Garrett wasn't... *involved* with him. Anne had dated a fellow for several months before she realized he was more interested in her bodyguard Gunter than her.

But Garrett was so masculine and virile.

Before she could work up the nerve to ask him, the owner of the voice appeared at the end of the hallway. His face was bruised and swollen and he leaned on a pair of crutches to take the weight off a leg that was encased in plaster from foot to midthigh. It was his friend from the hospital, she realized. The one who had been in the accident.

He walked toward them, the agony of each measured step clear on his poor battered face.

"Bloody hell, Ian!" Garrett barked in a tone Louisa had never heard him use. Like a father chastising a disobedient child. The way Chris had often spoken to her when she was younger. And sometimes still did. "The doctor said to stay off your feet as much as possible."

"Had to use the loo," the Ian person said with a wry smile, then he turned his attention to Louisa and opened his mouth to speak, but he must have recognized her because his jaw fell instead. He looked at Garrett and said, "Damn, that's the *Princess*."

Garrett cursed and shook his head, and when Ian just stood there gaping, he kicked him in his good leg and said, "Bow, you jackass."

"Sorry." He bowed his head, wearing a humble grin,

and said, "Must be all the pain medication they've pumped in me."

"Oh, it's all right," she assured him and offered a hand to shake. "Princess Louisa Josephine Elisabeth Alexander."

Balancing on one crutch, he took her hand, enfolding it in his rough, callused one and said, "I'm Ian. Ian Sutherland."

Nine

"Sutherland?" Louisa repeated, looking to Garrett, clearly confused. And why wouldn't she be when he'd told her this was an acquaintance who'd been in the accident. "You're related?"

Garrett cursed under his breath. Could this day possibly get any worse? He'd hoped to get Ian settled then leave him in the nurse's care and lock himself in his office for the rest of the day, but due to a scheduling snafu, the nurse wouldn't be coming until tomorrow morning.

And now, to top it all off, he had no choice but to tell Louisa the truth. "Ian is my brother."

"There's actually an uncanny family resemblance, when my face isn't all bruised and swollen," Ian told her. "Although I am the better looking one."

Louisa turned to Garrett, brow furrowed. "But you said—"

"I know. I lied."

This would normally be the time when Ian would jump in and say or do something to make Garrett look like even more of an ass, but instead he actually defended him. It was the least selfish thing Garrett had ever seen him do. "Compared to someone like me, Garrett here is a Boy Scout, Your Highness. If he did lie, I know he had a damned good reason."

She looked between Ian and Garrett as though she wasn't sure what to believe.

Though Ian would usually stick around for the fireworks, he yawned and said, "If you'll both excuse me, I'm feeling woozy from the pain medication. I think it's time for my afternoon nap. But I hope we'll get the chance to talk again, Your Highness."

"I'd like that," Louisa said with a smile, and as Ian limped back down the hall she turned to Garrett with a questioning look, as if to say, *Okay, what's the deal?*

"I know I owe you an explanation." He gestured to the staircase. "Let's go to my office, where we can talk in private."

She nodded and followed him up the stairs, but as they passed his bedroom, she stopped.

"This is your room?"

He nodded.

Without asking his permission, she stepped inside. She inhaled deeply and said, "Hmm, it smells like you."

He leaned in and sniffed, but to him it smelled the same way it always did. Just like the rest of the house.

He waited by the door for her to come out. Instead she dropped her purse on the floor, hoisted herself onto his bed and leaned back on her elbows, making herself comfortable. God, did she look sexy. She wore a sleeveless pink blouse and conservative white skirt, with her hair flowing loose and soft on her back. Maybe it was his imagination but it seemed the longer he knew her, the more attractive he found her.

She patted the mattress beside her, signaling him to sit down. Apparently they were having their talk right here.

He closed the door and crossed to the bed, taking a seat to her left. "Let me say first that I'm sorry I lied to you."

"When you first let me in and you looked so nervous, I thought maybe you were seeing another woman. Then I heard Ian's voice and for a second I thought maybe you were seeing a man."

The things that came out of her mouth never ceased to amaze him. "I told you before, Louisa, there's only you. And for the record, only *women*."

"Why didn't you tell me it was your brother in the accident?"

"Because I knew you would want to meet him."

"Is that such a bad thing?"

"Yes. Because he's a liar and a thief and I didn't want to expose you to someone like that. The only reason he came to see me is because my parents and my brothers have all written him off."

She frowned. "That's so sad."

"No, it isn't," he said, and told her some of the things Ian had done to the family, how he'd cheated and lied and stolen from them. And how Garrett was stuck with him now, until his leg healed. "He keeps telling me that he'll really change this time, but I've heard the story a hundred times before. People like that never change."

"But maybe this time he *really* means it."

"Do you know how he got into the accident? I told him I wouldn't give him money, so he stole my car instead."

"Are you sure he wasn't just borrowing it?"

"He admitted to stealing it, not to mention a dozen bottles of my best liquor. Then he tried to make me believe he'd had second thoughts and was bringing it back. But I know better. He left and had no intention of ever coming back."

"Yet you're letting him stay here," she said. "You must still care at least a little."

"I had no choice. He had nowhere else to go."

"If you really didn't care at all, that wouldn't have made a difference."

Though he hated to admit it, she had a point. But he didn't want her to be right. He wanted to hate Ian for all that he'd done. It was so much easier that way.

He groaned and flopped down on his back beside her.

"Stressed out?" she asked.

"Does it show?"

An impish smile curled her lips and he instantly knew she was up to no good. "You know what they say is supposed to be good for stress."

He had a few suggestions, but he was much more interested in her ideas. "Why don't you show me?"

She leaned over and brushed a soft, lingering kiss against his lips, then sat back and asked, "Better?"

Suppressing a smile, he shrugged and said, "A little, I guess."

Looking thoughtful, she said, "Hmm, maybe I'm just not trying hard enough."

She leaned over to give it another go, but he had a sudden revelation. "Hey, wait a minute."

She stopped abruptly and sat up. "What's wrong?"

"Something is missing."

She frowned. "What?"

He rose up on his elbows, looking around the room. "Security."

"Oh, they're here. They're outside, guarding the doors."

"Outside? As in, not inside?"

She looked at him funny. "Yes."

"And there's no chance of them possibly barging in and say, coming upstairs to this room?"

He could see by the slow smile creeping across her face that she knew where he was going with this. "Only if I ask them to. But what about your brother? Is there any reason he would come up here?"

"He's taking a nap. Besides, he can hardly walk, much less climb the stairs."

"You know what that means," she said.

They both smiled and said in unison, "We're finally alone."

Louisa was suddenly so excited her hands were trembling. "I have to be back to the hospital by seven for dinner."

He looked at his watch. "That gives us a little over two hours."

She thought of all the things they could do in two hours.

"Why don't you lie back against the pillows," Garrett said, and he had this look in his eyes, one that said, I'm going to eat you alive.

She realized that the dynamics had suddenly changed. A minute ago, when she was kissing Garrett, she had been the one in control. Now Garrett was clearly calling the shots, and though it scared her a little, it also thrilled her to the depths of her soul.

So why was she just sitting there wasting precious time?

Garrett regarded her curiously, "You're not getting cold feet, are you?"

She reached up and laid a hand on his cheek. "No! I want this, more than anything. It's all I've thought of for weeks. Maybe *too* much."

He leaned in and brushed a kiss against her lips and she could swear she felt it all the way down to her toes. "There's no such thing as too much."

"And that's the problem. Here we are alone, with no reason to stop if things start to go too far."

"How far is too far?"

"I know it's archaic and silly, but I want to be a virgin on my wedding night. I just think it will make it more special."

"It's not silly. It's an honorable decision, and knowing your wishes, I would never let things go too far."

His gaze was so earnest, she wanted to believe him, but who's to say he wouldn't get too carried away? "What if you can't stop?"

He grinned, his dimple winking at her. "Contrary to what you may have read, not all men are sex-starved fiends. You have my word that we won't go any further than we should."

She believed him, because she knew Garrett would never lie to her. At least, not about something so important. And when he had lied about Ian, he'd done it to protect her.

She sat up and scooted backward, laying her head on the pillow. Garrett lay down beside her and propped himself up on one elbow. He studied her face, softly tracing her features with his index finger. "Have I ever told you how beautiful you are?"

"Probably. But feel free to tell me again."

He kissed her instead. So tender and sweet—at first anyway. He kissed her lips and her chin and the side of her neck. He nibbled her earlobes and found a sensitive little spot behind her ear that made her shiver.

Her hesitance a memory now, she wrapped her arms around his neck, threaded her fingers through his hair, breathing in the scent of his skin and his hair. Feeding off his kisses.

Garrett cupped the side of her face, caressed her cheek with his thumb, but gradually his hand slipped lower, first down her throat and neck, then to her shoulder, but he stopped there.

A little voice inside of her was begging, *Keep going, please keep touching me.* Her breasts or even between her legs, anywhere that might relieve the ache building inside of her. It would be okay if he did, because he'd promised not to let this go too far, and she trusted him.

Maybe she was thinking loud enough for him to hear, because his hand started to move again, drifting slowly until it covered her breast. The ache between her thighs became a raging inferno, and her breasts felt swollen and tender. For a minute he just held his hand there, as though he worried she might be afraid—or he was trying to drive her mad. Louisa held her breath, anticipating his next move, and when he squeezed softly the sensation was so intense she gasped.

He stopped kissing her and gazed down with lust-filled eyes. "Too much?"

"No!" she said in a voice so husky with desire she barely recognized it as her own. "Not enough."

Wearing a sexy grin, he stroked one breast, then the other. When he took one nipple between his fingers and gently pinched, she whimpered. Men had touched her breasts before, but never had it felt this good. This... erotic.

Then he *stopped*. She opened her mouth to protest, but he started unbuttoning her blouse and the words died in her throat.

"I've been wondering something," he said, popping each button open with the flick of his skilled fingers. She watched as the last button gave way and he eased the sides back, exposing her pink lace bra. She wasn't particularly large, a modest B cup, but what she lacked in size, she made up for in quality.

"What were you wondering?" she asked.

"How inexperienced are you? I mean, you must have some experience."

"Some heavy petting, but always on top of the clothes. And kissing, of course."

"What kind of kissing?" he asked.

What kind? How many kinds were there?

Confused, she said, "Just regular kissing, I guess."

He flashed her an impish grin and she knew instantly that he was up to something.

"Anyone ever kiss you like this?" He dipped his head, brushing his lips on her breast at the very edge of the lace cup and Louisa could barely suppress the moan building in her throat. He kissed one, then the other, then he lifted his head to look at her.

"No," she answered in an unsteady voice. "Never like that."

"How about like this?" Using his tongue, he drew a damp path down the swell of one breast then up its mate. Then he looked at her and grinned.

Technically that wasn't a kiss, but this was no time to be splitting hairs. Kiss or not, she was so turned on she felt like crawling out of her own skin. "I'm going to have to say no. In fact, pretty much anything you do at this point will be new territory for me." And she could hardly wait to see where and how he touched her next. Fortunately she didn't have to wait long.

Garrett nudged the cup of her bra aside, and for a second all he did was look at her. Her nipple was small and pink and pulled tight with arousal.

"You have the most beautiful breasts I've ever seen," he said. She knew she should be polite and thank him, but he leaned forward and touched the very tip with his tongue and her brain went into shutdown mode. She didn't think anything could feel more erotic…until he drew her nipple into his mouth and sucked. Hard. She threw her head back and moaned, arching closer to his mouth.

He leaned back to look at his handiwork. Her nipple was damp and tinted deep red from the suction. She expected him to do the same to the other breast, but instead he gazed down at her, his expression serious, and said, "We should probably stop for now."

Wait, what? Was he serious? *"Stop?"*

"So things don't go too far."

She must have looked absolutely crestfallen, because he laughed and said, "Louisa, I'm teasing."

"Bloody hell, don't joke about a thing like that!" she scolded, expelling a relieved breath.

"We are running a little short on time."

She looked at his watch and couldn't believe how much time had passed already. And all they had done was kiss and touch. But she wanted more, and she wanted it now. If she was a little late for dinner, so be it. "Then let's not waste any more time."

She tugged on the hem of his shirt, and he helped her pull it over his head. His body was the most amazing she had ever seen and not just because his chest was wide and muscular, his abdomen hard and defined. She loved it because it belonged to him. She raised her hands and laid them on his chest, surprised by how hot his skin felt. Without his shirt to cover it, she could see his erection clearly against the loose jogging pants. So clearly that she realized he must not be wearing briefs or even boxers.

Garrett frowned and pressed one of his hands over hers. "You're shaking. Are you afraid?"

She shook her head. "Not at all. Just excited."

And fed up with going so slow.

She pushed Garrett onto his back, then sat up and straddled him, her skirt riding up all the way to the tops of her thighs. She shrugged out of her shirt then reached behind her and unclasped her bra, feeling an almost excruciating need to press her body to his, to rub her breasts against his chest. Garrett must have read her mind, because he seemed to know exactly what to do. As soon as her bra was off, he pulled her down to him, wrapping his arms around her. Their lips met in what was more of a mutual devouring than an actual kiss. They fed off one another, and if she could have eaten him alive, she would have.

Garrett's hands seemed to be everywhere at once. Up and down her back and arms, kneading her breasts, tangling in her hair. But when he reached under her skirt and cupped her behind in his big, warm hands, the ache between her legs became unbearable.

He rolled her onto her back, and it felt so good, the weight of his body on hers, lying chest to chest, stomach to stomach. She wrapped her legs around his waist, unaware until that very second that his erection had become pinned between them, centered perfectly in line with the crotch of her panties.

Louisa gasped with surprise and Garrett groaned, then they both went still, Garrett wearing an expression that suggested this time, they may have gone too far.

Technically this was her fault. Had she been more experienced, she would have anticipated this, and she knew they were tempting fate lying like this, with barely more than a thin layer of nylon and a swatch of lace to prevent this from going any further.

But it felt *so* good.

For several seconds they just stared at one another, as if neither was sure what to do next. She didn't relax her vise grip on his waist, and he didn't try to pull loose.

Then it happened. With his eyes locked on hers, Garrett rocked back then inched slowly forward, stroking her with the entire length of his erection. Louisa felt it like an electric charge that started between her thighs and raced outward. She shuddered involuntarily and all the fine hairs on her body shivered to life.

He did it again, but this time she arched up to meet

him and every inch of her skin, every cell in her body overflowed with pleasure, even though they still had their clothes on.

Garrett rocked into her, over and over, with the same slow, measured thrusts and her body moved naturally with him. She kissed his lips and his throat, bit his earlobes and raked her nails across his back and shoulders. She wanted to eat him up, brand him with her teeth and her nails. Not the way a proper princess should behave. But she didn't care. She felt naughty and sexy and half out of her mind with lust, his every thrust driving her closer and closer to ecstasy.

So close.

She looked up at Garrett. His eyes were closed, his breath ragged and sweat beaded his forehead. For some reason she'd thought he was doing this just to make her feel good, but in that instant she realized that he was going to climax, and that was all it took to drive her past the point of no return. Everything locked and a shudder that started in her center rippled out to encompass her entire being. She would have moaned but she couldn't breathe, couldn't even think past the numbing pleasure.

Feeling her climax must have done Garrett in. He groaned from deep within his chest then went rigid, hissing out a breath as he gave one final thrust then dropped beside her.

Ten

Louisa lay beside Garrett in his bed, limp and trying to catch her breath, and suddenly, for no reason, Garrett started to laugh. A deep throaty laugh, as though he found something about the situation profoundly amusing.

"What's so funny?" she asked.

He gazed up at the ceiling, shaking his head. "I can't believe we just did that."

She frowned. "Was it…bad?"

He rolled onto his side, rising up on one elbow to look at her. "No, not at all. It was…fantastic."

She was confused. "So why are you laughing?"

"Because the last time I did it that way I was fifteen. It's a bit like wet dreams. After a certain age, you just don't have them."

She nodded thoughtfully. "I guess that makes sense."

"What do you mean?"

"Well, despite all the stories I've read, I've never seen any mention of what we just did."

He grinned. "You would if they were written by adolescent boys."

"So what we did was…unusual?"

"Very. It usually takes actual intercourse for me to climax."

"Why is that, do you think?"

He shrugged. "I guess, once you start having sex, the novelty gradually wears off. But you turn me on so much, it's like being a kid again. Starting from the beginning."

That might have been one of the sweetest things a man had ever said to her. She grinned and said, "Think we could do it again?"

"Have you looked at the time?"

She read the display on his watch. Damn! It was already half past six. But if she hurried she could make it on time for dinner. "I'm sorry. I do have to go."

"I understand."

He looked so sexy lying there with no shirt on, wearing that adorable smile. She didn't want to leave. She wanted to curl into his chest and cuddle with him. She wanted to fall asleep in his bed and wake in his arms, but she knew that her family was expecting her. And if she didn't show, those guards who were waiting patiently outside might just break down the door to fetch her.

She rolled out of bed and grabbed her clothes.

Garrett lay there and watched her dress. "I have a grueling day at the office tomorrow, but maybe I could see you in the evening."

"Oh, I can't. I forgot to tell you, I'm filling in for

Chris at some executive dinner. Now that he's finally taking me seriously, I couldn't refuse. What about the night after that?"

"Friday? I have a dinner meeting."

"Do you have work to do Saturday?"

"If I do, it will have to wait. What would you like to do?"

Did he even have to ask?

Well, for propriety's sake she could at least *pretend* they weren't getting together just to ravish each other. "It might be difficult going out on an actual date," she reminded him. "With all the security issues."

"True," he agreed thoughtfully. "I suppose we could just stay indoors."

"I'm sure we could figure out *something* to keep us occupied."

He smiled that sexy smile and asked, with a voice full of sexual innuendo, "Your place or mine?"

They decided to meet at his place, since here they would have the least interruption, then Garrett walked Louisa to the door. She called her bodyguard to let him know she was ready, and through the front window Garrett could see that there was a slew of vehicles parked in the street in front of his town house.

"The media circus has begun," he told her.

She peered around him to see. "It sort of comes with the territory. But you get used to it. Once they have their photos and press releases, the hype will die down."

He hoped so. He preferred to keep his life low profile—one more thing he would sacrifice as Louisa's husband. Though he had a feeling, for a while at least, she would make up for it in *other* ways. And right now she looked so damned adorable, all rumpled and sexy, he wanted to drag her back upstairs.

There was a knock on the door and Garrett opened it to find two hulking bodyguards on his porch, the same ones from the hospital. Garrett was a big man, but these guys were giants, and he had little doubt Louisa would be quite safe in their care.

"We're ready, Your Highness," the one on the left said.

Louisa turned to Garrett, rose up on her toes and pressed a kiss to his lips, then she smiled and said, "See you Saturday."

As soon as her foot hit the step, he heard the dull roar of camera shutters firing away and reporters shouting questions from the street. Even knowing he would be tomorrow's fodder for the tabloids, he stood there and watched as she was helped in the car. She waved as the car pulled away and he waved back, watching until they rounded the corner at the end of the block. Then he heard from behind him, "My big brother, shagging a princess."

He closed the door and turned to find Ian standing a few feet away, at the end of the hallway.

"Who I 'shag' is none of your concern. And for the record, I'm not."

"Maybe, but you will be, because you always get what you want." Ian shook his head and laughed. "Leave it to Garrett the overachiever to set his sights on the royal family."

Garrett glared at him and walked past Ian to the kitchen to get himself a beer. If Ian hadn't cleaned him out already, that is.

Ian followed him.

Surprisingly, there was the same number of bottles as the night before. Garrett took one out and twisted off the cap.

"Aren't you going to offer me some?" Ian asked.

"Pain pills and alcohol. Smashing combination." He closed the refrigerator.

Ian leaned back against the counter and propped his crutches in the corner. "I knew you were a power hound, but I never imagined you had the stones to bag a princess. What do you think Mum and Dad would say?"

"Since they're not talking to me, I don't imagine they would say much of anything."

"I thought families were supposed to have only one black sheep," Ian said with a wry smile, but Garrett could swear he saw regret lurking behind his eyes.

Was it possible that he had a conscience after all? That he really did want to change?

Garrett washed the possibility away with a swallow of ale. If he let himself get his hopes up, he would only be disappointed later.

"He's jealous, you know," Ian said.

"Who?"

"Our father."

Garrett frowned. "Jealous of whom?"

"You."

He had no idea what Ian was talking about. His father had made it very clear that he wanted nothing to do with Garrett or his money. "That's ridiculous."

"It's true. He was never what you would call a pleasant man, we both have the scars to prove that, but after you left for university things were bad."

Garrett automatically reached up to touch the small scar at the corner of his mouth. From a crack in the jaw he'd received for staying late at school to finish a project when he should have been home doing his chores. "How bad?"

"His temper became even more volatile. I had never seen him so angry. He and Mum were fighting all the time. But you know Mum, she would take it all. I was just a kid, but even I knew that wasn't right. I asked her one day why he hated us so much."

Garrett couldn't help but ask, "What did she say?"

"That he was an unhappy man. That he had dreams of going to university and doing more with his life, but being the oldest, it was his responsibility to take over the farm when his father retired. And he did it, because that was what was expected of him. He married and became a farmer, just like he was supposed to. He settled. Then you came along, knowing exactly what you wanted and not letting a single thing get in your way. He envied you, Garrett, maybe even hated you for it, because that's the kind of man he was. And he convinced everyone else that what you'd done was some sort of slight against the family."

And here Garrett had always believed his father had been content as a farmer, that he was happy with the simple life he'd chosen. "He never once said a word about wanting anything different."

Ian shrugged. "It wasn't his way."

"Even if I knew, it wouldn't have changed anything. I still would have left."

"I'm not blaming you, Garrett. I just thought you should know why he's such a bastard. I mean, at least I *deserve* the family's hatred. You haven't done anything wrong."

"A father should want better for his sons. He should

want them to strive for more. Instead he was always trying to hold me back."

"That's his problem, not yours."

So why did Garrett still feel like it was his fault? Like he'd done something wrong? Parents were supposed to love their kids unconditionally. Push them to succeed. And it wasn't just his father at fault. His mum bore just as much blame. She should have defended Garrett, should have been his advocate, not her husband's enabler.

Like Ian said, it wasn't Garrett's fault. But he couldn't decide if this new information was a relief or only made him feel worse.

How many times had he told himself that he'd stopped caring? That nothing they could say or do could hurt him, even if that meant them not saying or doing anything at all? Somewhere deep down, did he still care?

He took a long swallow, draining the bottle, then said, "Shouldn't you be lying down resting or something?"

"I'm bored," Ian said. "She's really nice by the way."

"Who?"

"Who?" Ian laughed. "The *Princess*. Your girlfriend. The one you aren't shagging. Who did you think I meant?"

His brother had just informed him that everything he knew about his life was untrue, so it was natural for Garrett to be a bit confused. "Yes, she is."

"I'll bet she's a handful though."

He narrowed his eyes at his brother. "Why would you say that?"

"Mischief recognizes mischief. And honestly, I think that's exactly the kind of woman you need. One who won't give you the chance to be bored."

It surprised Garrett how well Ian knew him. Ian had been so young when Garrett left. So carefree. Maybe there was more going on in his head than people realized.

Garrett had left his phone on the counter and it began to ring. Before he could reach for it, Ian grabbed it. Rather than hand it to Garrett, he answered himself. He greeted the caller just the way Garrett would, then for several seconds just listened. At first Garrett thought it might be some sort of automated call, then Ian said, "Sorry, I think it's Garrett you want to speak to." With another wry smile he handed the phone to Garrett. "It's a fellow named Wes. He called to say that he saw you on the news just now and it looks as though the situation with the Princess is going just as planned."

Bloody hell. Ian knew. Not specifically what, but he knew Garrett was up to something. And he wouldn't hesitate to hold it against him.

Garrett took the phone. "Wes?"

"Christ, Garrett, was that Ian? He sounds just like you."

"Yes, it was."

"I'm sorry. If I had known…"

"Don't worry about it."

"I called to tell you that I just saw footage on the telly of her leaving your place."

That was quick. "It was something of a media frenzy outside."

"Well, you certainly gave them fodder to chew on."

Garrett frowned. "What do you mean?"

Wes told him about the footage he'd seen and Garrett groaned. Suddenly what Ian did or didn't know was inconsequential.

"I take it that wasn't deliberate," Wes said.

No, and he had the feeling he would be hearing from Chris regarding the matter, if the family hadn't banished him from the castle, from Louisa's life, already.

"I'm here!" Louisa called cheerily as she breezed into Melissa's hospital room at seven on the nose...and was met by total silence.

Melissa reclined in bed and Chris stood beside her, arms crossed over his chest. Aaron and Liv sat in chairs across the room by the window, and Anne was seated across from them. And they all just stared at her.

Did they know what she'd been up to?

Of course not. She had looked a bit rumpled when she left Garrett's town house but she'd fixed her makeup and hair in the car. "What? Why are you looking at me like that?"

"We saw you on the telly," Anne remarked with a smirk.

Was *that* all? They were always on television for some reason or another. It's not as though her relationship with Garrett was some kind of secret.

She shrugged and asked, "So?"

Everyone exchanged a look, then Melissa said, "You looked a little...disheveled."

Yes, she probably should have fixed up herself before she left, but it wasn't that big of a deal. "So my hair wasn't perfect. Is it really the end of the world?"

"Well," Liv began, looking pained. "There was your shirt, too."

"What about it?" she asked, and Liv gestured for her to see for herself.

Louisa looked down and her heart sank. She must

have been in quite a rush when she dressed because she'd fastened the buttons on her blouse cockeyed.

"Oops." She turned away and swiftly fixed it.

"I guess this means you blew that vow to be a virgin on your wedding night," Anne snipped, and Louisa spun to face her. That was supposed to be private, a secret shared between sisters.

"What's your problem?" Louisa said, so tired of Anne dumping on her that she wanted to scream.

Anne just sneered. "Should we expect a shotgun wedding, or were you smart enough to use a condom?"

"Anne!" Chris cut in sharply.

"I wish you would do something to kill the bug that has crawled up your you-know-where, so I could have my sister back," Louisa retorted. "And not that it's yours or anyone else's business, but I am still pure as the driven snow." More or less.

"That may be true," Aaron said, "but it looked as though you'd spent the afternoon shagging."

She could understand why people might get that impression, and why Chris looked so disappointed in her. "It was an accident," she told him.

"Yes, well, it's not the kind of thing that someone would do on purpose. All that tells me is that you were being careless."

"I was in a hurry. I was running late and wanted to get here on time. If I had taken the time to fix myself up, I would have been late and you would have chastised me for that." No matter what she did, she couldn't win.

"Then you should have taken that into consideration and stopped whatever it was you were doing earlier to give yourself extra time. With everything else we have to worry about, this is the last thing the family needs, Louisa. It reflects badly on me."

Him? "How did this become about *you?*"

"Because it is my responsibility to hold this family together in our father's absence. How do you think he and Mother will feel when they see this on the news? Who do you think they'll blame?"

She hadn't thought about it like that. She bit her lip and lowered her eyes, suddenly filled with shame. "I'm sorry."

Sometimes she forgot how much pressure Chris must be under. First taking over their father's duties, and now having Melissa in the hospital and his children's health at risk. He was right. She was being irresponsible and selfish.

"I'm sending Anne to speak for me tomorrow," he told her, twisting the knife in a little deeper. Prince Chris giveth, then he taketh away.

She nodded, unable to meet his eyes. "I understand."

Not only had she let him and the rest of the family down, but the way Anne had been acting lately, she would take satisfaction rubbing this in Louisa's face.

"You *will* be more careful next time," he said, and she went limp with relief. At least he wasn't going to put her on house arrest, or insist she stop seeing Garrett. He was giving her another chance.

"I will," she told him. "I promise."

Her cell phone started to ring and she practically dove into her purse to grab it. It was Garrett's number. "I need to get this," she told Chris.

He nodded, signaling what she hoped was the end of

the tongue-lashing. At least for now, but God forbid she screw up again. Chris wouldn't be so lenient. He might do something drastic, like lock her in a tower and never let her out.

Eleven

Louisa escaped into the waiting room and answered her phone. "Hi."

"Did I get you at a bad time?" Garrett asked.

"No, your timing was perfect. Chris just finished chastising me to within an inch of my life," she said, and could swear she felt him cringe.

"I take it they saw the news clip."

"Yeah. Did you?"

"Yeah. A friend called to tell me so I put the television on. It's been on practically every channel, so it was hard to miss."

She tensed up. "Aaron said I looked like I spent the afternoon shagging."

"Yeah, you did. I'm sorry."

"Why are you apologizing?"

"Because I never should have let you leave my house. As you were getting ready to walk out the door I was thinking to myself how mussed you looked, but I just thought it was sexy as hell. It never occurred to me that the press would notice, too."

"What about my blouse?"

"That I honestly didn't notice or I would have told you." He paused then asked, "Chris was angry?"

"It was more of an I'm-not-angry-I'm-disappointed speech. And to be honest, anger would have been a lot easier to stomach. I feel terrible. I promised him that next time I would be more careful."

"Does that mean we're still on for Saturday?"

"Definitely. Although there was a point when I worried he might stick me on permanent house arrest. And coincidentally, I'm also free Thursday, as well. Chris asked Anne to sit in for him instead. I guess he doesn't trust me."

"Well, I made plans with my friend Wes to golf that evening, but I could cancel."

She shelved her disappointment. "No, don't do that. I don't want to be *that girl*."

"What girl?"

"The one who makes her boyfriend drop all of his friends and monopolizes his every waking moment. Go golfing and have fun. I'll see you Saturday."

The hospital room door opened and Anne stepped through. She shot a quick, nervous glance at Louisa then walked to the ladies' room. What was her deal?

"Are you sure? Because I know he would understand."

"I'm sure. I have plenty to keep me busy." She loved the idea that he wanted to be with her, but she needed to let him have some normalcy before things got too serious between them, because eventually he was bound to become a target for the Gingerbread Man and security would become an issue for him, as well. He should enjoy his freedom while he still could. "Maybe you could call me before you go to bed," she suggested.

"Eleven too late?"

"I'll keep the phone beside me just in case I drift off." Maybe they could even give that phone sex thing a try. She was about to mention it when she heard what sounded like retching from the ladies' room. Was Anne sick?

"Garrett, I have to let you go," she said. "I'll talk to you tomorrow."

They said their goodbyes and she walked over to the door to listen. It was quiet for a minute, then she heard the unmistakable sound echoing off the tile walls. She knocked on the door. "Anne, are you okay?"

"I'm fine," she called back, but immediately the vomiting started again. It sounded violent and painful, and Louisa started to actually worry something was seriously wrong.

"Do you need anything?" she asked.

"No. Go away."

She sighed. She was trying to help and Anne was still copping an attitude. "Would you stop being such a bitch and let me in? For reasons I cannot begin to comprehend, I'm worried about you!"

A few seconds passed and she heard the toilet flush, then the lock on the door snapped and Anne yelled, "You can come in."

She opened the door, taken aback by what she found. Anne was sitting on the floor near the commode, her cheek resting against the tile wall. A sheen of sweat dampened her face, and aside from two bright red patches on her cheeks, all the color had leeched from her skin.

Alarmed, Louisa stepped inside and shut the door. "What's wrong? Are you sick?"

She shook her head. "I'm fine."

"You are *not* fine." She reached down to feel her forehead, but Anne batted her hand away.

"I don't have a fever."

"If you're sick, you shouldn't be anywhere near Melissa."

"I told you I'm not sick."

Then what other explanation—

"Oh my God, are you bulimic?"

Anne laughed weakly. "Louisa, bulimics vomit *after* they eat. Not before."

"If you're not sick and you're not bulimic, what's going on? Healthy people don't throw up like that."

"Some healthy *women* do," Anne said.

It took a minute, but the meaning of her words finally sank in and Louisa gasped. "Oh my God," she hissed in a loud whisper. "Are you *pregnant?*"

"You can't tell *anyone,*" Anne said.

"Oh my God," she said again, hardly able to believe it.

"Imagine how I felt when I took the pregnancy tests," Anne joked weakly.

"You took more than one?"

"I took five. I wanted to be sure."

That would definitely do it. "How far along are you?

"Just a few weeks."

"How did this happen?"

Anne raised a brow at her.

Louisa rolled her eyes. "Of course I know *how,* but when, and with whom? I didn't even know you were seeing anyone."

"I'm not. And the father is out of the picture. He doesn't want the baby or me."

"Are you sure?"

"*Very* sure."

"Oh, Anne, I'm so sorry." She sat down on the floor beside her sister and took her hand. She half expected her to pull away, but she didn't. At least this explained why Anne had been so cranky lately. Her hormones must have been raging, and to top it off, having the father reject her and the baby? She must have been devastated.

"Who is it, Anne?"

"It's not important."

"Yes, it is. Someone needs to make him own up to his responsibility."

"I'm not even sure what *I'm* going to do yet."

Louisa's heart skipped. "You don't mean...?"

"What I mean is, I haven't decided if I'm going to keep it, or give it up for adoption. If I choose adoption, I figure I can hold out until it's impossible to hide, then take an extended vacation. No one will have to know a thing."

That would be tough enough for an average woman to pull off, but a princess? Someone was bound to figure it out. "You don't want to have children?"

"Not like this. Besides, look how everyone reacted to you leaving your boyfriend's house looking a little untidy. Can you imagine how they would take the news of me having a child out of wedlock? I'm not sure Daddy could take the stress of a huge scandal right now."

She hadn't heard Anne call him "Daddy" in years. "He'll be okay."

Anne shook her head, looking troubled. "He doesn't look good, Louisa. He's lost so much weight and he has so little energy now. You should have seen the look on his face when the doctor said there was so little improvement. He was devastated. And Mum is a total wreck. I think she sees the same thing I do."

"What's that?"

"I think he's giving up."

Louisa shook her head. "He would never do that. He's strong."

"He's been so sick and in and out of hospitals for so long. I think he's just tired."

"I can't accept that."

"I know you love him. We all do, and I think right now he's holding on for us. But there is going to come a time when we have to let go. We have to let him know that it's okay to stop fighting."

She knew she was being selfish, but she didn't *want* him to stop fighting. He was going to walk her down the aisle at her wedding and be there to play with her children. She simply could not imagine her life without him in it. "How do you know he's ready to quit? Did he tell you?"

"He didn't have to. I just knew. I think you will, too. When you're ready."

She didn't know if she would *ever* be ready for that.

There was a soft rap at the door, startling them both.

"Come in," Anne called.

The door opened a crack and Liv stuck her head in, she looked around, then her gaze dropped and she frowned. "Oh, there you are. We thought maybe you'd left. Why are you sitting on the floor?"

"Hot flashes," Anne said. "Damned PMS. I thought it would be cooler down here."

It was the dumbest excuse Louisa had ever heard, but Liv didn't question it.

"Oh. Well, dinner is getting cold."

Louisa smiled. "Thanks, we'll be right in."

Liv shot them one last odd look that suggested her sisters-in-law were both a few beakers short of a complete lab, then disappeared. It probably did look odd, the two of them alone in the bathroom sitting on the floor and holding hands no less.

"I really like her," Anne said, "but she's way too uptight. Maybe she just needs a good shag."

"That's definitely not the problem," Louisa said, and to Anne's how-do-*you*-know look, she added, "My room is right down the hall, and suffice it to say they aren't exactly quiet. And for the record, I really didn't sleep with Garrett. I want to though. I'm not sure I can wait until my wedding night."

"I'm sorry for what I said, Louisa. About your virginity. That was rotten of me. And I'm sorry I've been such a bitch lately."

"Under the circumstances I guess I can cut you some slack." She looked at Anne and smiled. "I'm just glad to have my sister back."

Anne gave her hand a squeeze. "I think I'm just jealous that you found someone you care about. I should be happy for you, not trying to drag you down."

"You don't still think he's using me?"

She shrugged. "What the hell do I know? If I was so

damned smart I wouldn't have gotten myself into this mess."

"It'll be okay, Annie," she assured her, using the nickname from their childhood. Anne was Annie, and Louisa was Lulu. She wondered when they had stopped that, when they felt they were too mature or too refined for silly names. They used to be silly a lot back then, and Louisa missed that. Sometimes she wished they could go back to those days when things were so simple and uncomplicated.

Or maybe it was all relative. Problems that seemed enormous back then were, in retrospect, not such a big deal now.

"You ready?" Anne asked.

She nodded and asked, "You?"

Balancing on the wall, she pushed herself to her feet. "May as well get this over with."

Louisa followed her out, thinking that maybe the trick was going back over all the experiences she'd had up until this point—the good times and bad times, the hurts and the happiness—and starting fresh.

Of course, going back would mean leaving Garrett forever, and that wasn't something she would ever do.

The headline of the morning paper was brutal. Clever, but brutal.

"Has Snow White Drifted?"

The photo beneath it was even worse. It was a shot of her being ushered to the car, her hair messy, her makeup all but gone. And of course there was the sloppily buttoned shirt, which the paper had conveniently circled for their readers' viewing ease. Under that was a smaller photo of Garrett standing at his front doorway in bare feet, his hair a mess and his clothes wrinkled.

"We *do* look like we've been shagging," she told Garrett.

"It's not *that* bad. For all the press knows, we could have been out for a run."

She tossed the paper off the bed and switched the phone to her other ear. "Yes, I often run in a skirt and sandals."

"My point is, no one can know for sure *what* we were doing. Besides us, of course. Now if we'd made a sex tape that was leaked to the press…"

"Bite your tongue," she said and he laughed.

"Don't worry. It'll blow over."

She wondered how his family was reacting to the press. But he'd already told her that he no longer spoke to them.

"When was the last time you talked to your father?" she asked.

Her question seemed to surprise him. "Where did that come from?"

"I've been thinking about family a lot lately. I was just curious."

"I haven't spoken to him since the day I purchased his land."

"You bought his farm?"

"It was the first piece of property I ever owned. They were in trouble. They had a bad crop, and with their debt, he wasn't able to pay his taxes. The land was about to be seized and put up for auction. I bought it, thinking that I would present it to him as a gift. He and my mum could live there until the day he died and never have to worry about money again."

"He must have been so grateful."

"He tore the deed in half and threw it back in my face. He told me that I was no longer his son."

Louisa gasped. "He didn't!"

"He said he didn't want my charity."

The idea that he would do that to his son made Louisa's heart ache. And all Garrett had done was try to help. "You must have felt horrible."

"My father was always a proud man, but I admit I never expected that reaction. I thought he would finally see that my choice to go to college had paid off. That I'd made the right decision. He always told me that the land would someday be mine. I guess that only applied if I became a farmer like him. Instead he preferred that it be purchased off the auction block by some stranger rather than by his own flesh and blood."

Tears shimmered in her eyes. "I can't imagine how much that must have hurt you."

"It was a feeling of resignation more than anything. And maybe in a way a relief. He had drawn his line in the sand. I could finally stop trying to please him."

"You at least tried to talk to him, didn't you?"

"There wasn't much point. He made his feelings clear."

"But…he's your father. I'm sure he still loves you."

"Well, it's too late now."

"It's never too late, Garrett. If you don't at least try to heal the rift between you and he dies, it will haunt you for the rest of your life."

"Why this sudden interest in my family?"

"Anne told me something about our father the other day, and…" Tears welled up in her eyes again and she swallowed back a sob.

"Is something wrong?" he asked.

"It's not looking good." She told Garrett what Anne had said, and it took every ounce of energy she had not to fall apart.

Garrett figured he would be relishing the news of the King's permanent vacation from the throne. Because even if he didn't die, it sounded as though he would never be healthy enough to rule again. Which meant that Garrett was a shoo-in for that position Louisa had mentioned. At the very least, Garrett should have been relieved that finally all of his hard work was going to reap benefits.

Instead he felt like a piece of garbage.

He used to see the royal family as nothing more than an obstacle. A united front made up of faceless individuals he was determined to conquer. That attitude had suited him just fine—until he'd gotten to know them. Now everything had changed, and the idea that he could have been so greedy and shallow, so manipulative, disturbed him deeper than he could have imagined. He used to be a good person. He used to have principles, used to care about people.

He was revolted by the man he had become.

But he couldn't deny that he was really starting to care about Louisa. When she told him about the situation with her father, her voice so full of grief and fear, Garrett would have moved heaven and earth to take away her pain. To make it better. And quite frankly, it scared the hell out of him.

He didn't have time for attachments like that, time to worry himself with other people's baggage. He preferred to keep his life simple and uncomplicated.

And by choosing Louisa, that was what he believed he was getting. A sweet, demure, shell of a woman who would be easily manipulated and more or less trained to be exactly the kind of wife he wanted. The less seen and heard, the better.

Instead he got a feisty, passionate and independent woman. One who was about as likely to follow his "rules" as he was to don a tutu and become a ballerina.

Maybe she was his punishment for all his selfishness, his ruthless attitude. The thing is, she didn't *feel* like a punishment. Was it possible that she might actually be a blessing in disguise?

Twelve

Louisa lay in bed most of the night, tossing and turning, her mind working a million miles an hour. The idea of losing their father, and the possibility of Anne giving up her baby, was almost too much for her to bear. There was nothing much she could do for her father but be there to support him. And she could only do the same for Anne.

Early the following morning, she went to Anne's room to check on her. Louisa knocked, and when Anne answered she looked like death warmed over.

"Feeling sick?"

"Does it show?" Anne asked wryly, letting her in, then she crawled back into bed and burrowed under the covers.

"Is there anything I can do?"

She shook her head. "What's up?"

"I was wondering if you had decided what to do."

"About the baby, you mean?"

Louisa nodded and sat on the edge of the bed.

"Not definitively, but I'm leaning toward adoption. I'm just...I'm not ready to do this. Not this way. Besides, I would be a terrible single mother. I'm pessimistic and difficult. The baby would be much better off with someone else. Someone more...maternal. I'm just not cut out to be a mother."

"Of course you are! You would be a wonderful mother."

Anne shook her head. "Not now. Not like this."

Louisa wished there was something she could say to change her mind, but who was she to tell her sister how to live?

"What happened to this family, Anne? How did everything get all screwed up and turned around?"

"It just...happens. Things can't stay the same forever."

But she wanted them to. She wanted everything to go back to the way it used to be, when they were all healthy and happy and safe. Now it was just so...confusing. It seemed that the only really good thing in her life right now was Garrett. He made her happy. But it was a sort of happy she had never experienced before. Not with a man, anyway. When she was with him, she felt excited and hopeful and content all at once.

"Just for the record," Anne said, "I actually think you and Garrett will be really happy together."

"I think...I think I love him."

Anne regarded her curiously. "You sound surprised. From the second you met him, you've been so sure he was the one."

"I know, but that was different."

"Different how?"

"Let's face it, I've said I 'loved' at least a dozen other men before him. And yes, when I met Garrett I was convinced it was love at first sight. He was so dark and mysterious and sexy. But now that I've gotten to know him, the *real* him, I realize how immature and shallow those feelings really were. He's so much more than what I expected. And what I feel for him now is so much bigger than anything I've felt before. Complex and confusing and...wonderful."

"That's a good thing, right?"

"I hope so. A week ago I was absolutely certain that we were perfect for each other, that it was destiny. But what if I was wrong? What if I fell in love with him, but he doesn't love me back?"

"And what if he does?"

That would be wonderful, of course. "You know, the great thing about being naive is that you don't think about stuff like this. It's so much easier existing in a bubble, convinced life is wonderful and everything will work out."

"Yeah, but you can't live like that forever. Eventually the bubble will burst."

Maybe that was what had happened to her. Maybe her bubble had finally burst, because for the first time in her life she didn't have all the answers. She didn't believe that everything would be okay.

"By the way, as soon as I can manage to crawl out of bed, I'm telling Chris that I can't fill in for him anymore. Last night was miserable. Not only did I feel as though any second I would toss all over the podium, but when it comes to public speaking, you're just better than me.

You're in your element when you're interacting with people, and let's face it, I'm not."

"What if he says no?"

"I won't give him a choice. It's you or Aaron, and we both know Aaron won't want to do it."

After so many years of wanting her family to take her more seriously, to give her more responsibility, suddenly she was afraid. What if she wasn't good enough? What if she made another mistake?

She'd spent so much time whining and complaining and never had the slightest clue how easy she had it.

Technically she had been an adult for nine years, but until recently, she hadn't really grown up. She felt as though now it was finally time. But to grow up she would have to face one of her biggest fears. The one thing she'd been stalwartly avoiding.

"I have to go call Garrett," she told Anne.

"Is everything okay? You look…I don't know, like you're up to something." She frowned suddenly then asked, "You're not going to do something drastic are you?"

Drastic for Louisa maybe. "Everything is fine," she promised. Or at least, as close to fine as it could be under the circumstances.

Louisa dialed Garrett's home number, but he didn't answer.

She was about to try his cell when Geoffrey knocked on her door. "You have a visitor, Your Highness."

A visitor? This early? Then she realized it could be only one person. She raced to the door and flung it open. Garrett stood on the other side. He was dressed for work, a shy grin on his face. He looked delicious.

"Surprise," he said.

"Thank you, Geoffrey," Louisa said, grabbing Garrett's hand and tugging him into her room. The instant the door was closed she was in his arms. She must have looked a fright, still in her pajamas with her hair mussed, but she was so happy to see him she didn't care.

"I know it's early. I hope I didn't wake you."

"No, I've been up awhile." She pressed her cheek to his suit jacket, breathed in the scent of his aftershave. "And even if I had been asleep, I couldn't think of a better way to wake up."

He kissed the top of her head. "I've missed you, Princess."

Her heart overflowed with happiness. "I've missed you, too. But how did you get Geoffrey to bring you up here?"

"I lied and said you were expecting me. I know I'll see you tonight, but I didn't want to wait that long."

She really didn't want to do this, but she had to. "I was wondering if you would be upset if I cancelled our date."

"I guess that would depend on why you want to cancel it."

"I keep thinking about what Anne said, about our father. If she's right, I may not have a lot of time left with him. Not only that, but I think I need to see him for myself, but he's going to be in England for at least another week. Maybe longer. I'm thinking I should go stay with him. Just a few days."

"I think that's a good idea," he said.

She looked up at him. "You do?"

He touched her cheek. "Louisa, he's your father. Of course he should come first."

"I would leave this afternoon and fly back either Wednesday or Thursday."

"Take all the time you need. I'll still be here when you get back."

"You promise?"

He smiled. "I promise."

"Have I told you how wonderful you are?"

"Yeah, but you can tell me again." There was a smile in his voice, and it made her smile, too. "I suppose this means our trip to Cabo will have to wait awhile?"

"Are you angry?"

"Of course not."

She got up on her toes to press a kiss to his lips. "You're wonderful, and I'm going to miss you."

"You won't be on a different planet. We can still talk on the phone."

"I'd like that. In fact, if it's as bad as Anne has led me to believe, I might just need someone to talk to."

"In that case, I promise I'll call you every night."

"I'm terrified of what I'm going to find when I get there."

"Whatever it is, you'll deal with it. You're stronger than you give yourself credit for, you know."

She hoped so. "It would be so much harder going through this alone. I'm glad I met you, Garrett."

"You wouldn't be alone. You have your family."

"Yes, but they don't see me the way you do. They don't really listen to me, or take me seriously. But I know that you really care how I feel. I don't know what I would do without you."

"You never have to worry about that," he said.

She wondered if that was his way of saying that he wanted to marry her without actually saying it. But the truth was, right now she didn't care what it meant. She was just thankful to have him.

"How much time have you got?" she asked him.

He glanced at his watch. "A few minutes. Why?"

She slid her hands under his jacket and up his chest. "Well, since we won't see each other for several days, I thought we could spend some quality time together."

He grinned. "Oh, did you?"

"But if you only have a few minutes…"

He looped his arms around her and walked her backward toward the bed. "I'll make time," he growled, his eyes dark with desire.

Though he did eventually make it to work, he was very late.

Garrett did call her, just as he'd promised, and thank goodness she had him to talk to. Because things weren't as bad as Anne described. They were worse.

In the week he had been gone, it seemed as if her father had aged a decade. He was thin and sallow, as though the life had been sucked out of him, and when she embraced him, he felt frail. Gone was the strong and vibrant king. The leader. And in that instant she knew, without a shadow of a doubt, that he would never be coming back. Anne had been right. He'd lost his will to fight. His desire to live. It was a matter of time now.

Oddly enough, the person she felt more sorry for was her mother. She looked utterly exhausted and so brittle that with the slightest agitation, she could easily shatter.

"So, tell me about this new man of yours," her father

said, trying to sound jovial, but his voice was thready and weak.

"He's wonderful. He's handsome and smart and fun."

"Sounds like me," he said with a wink. "I'm anxious to meet him. I've heard good things from your brother."

It was odd, because this courtship hadn't been at all what she had imagined. She had expected it to be like a dream, like a fairy tale come true. Garrett would ride in like a knight in shining armor and whisk her away to a fantasy land. He would wine and dine her and take her on exotic trips. But thanks to security, they hadn't even had an actual date! And he hadn't showered her with lavish gifts and attention, like other men. He hadn't treated her like royalty at all. He'd treated her like…a person. And the strange thing was, she liked it. By acting the opposite of what she had expected, he'd won her heart.

"I know I've said this before about other men, but I really think he's the one. I…I like the way I feel when I'm with him. I like who I am."

"And who is that?" her mother asked.

"*Me*. And he seems to appreciate me for who I am."

"Are you saying I might finally get to walk one of my daughters down the aisle?" her father asked.

"It looks that way," she said, and oh, how she hoped he could. But if he couldn't be there physically, she knew he would be there in spirit. In her heart. "He hasn't actually asked yet, but I have this feeling it might be soon."

"You'll let us know the minute he does?" her mother prompted.

"I promise."

They chatted for a while, her parents carrying on as if everything was fine. They asked how Melissa was feeling, and how Chris was adjusting to having her away from home. They asked about Liv's research and if Aaron was still assisting her in the lab. They even asked about Muffin, who Louisa had left in the care of Elise, one of the maids. She had small children who loved to play with and pamper him, and an elderly mother who adored him. Of course Muffin, being a total attention hound, was in his glory. He needed someone who had more time to devote to him. Louisa confessed to her parents that as much as she loved him, in light of everything that was happening lately, she might let Elise keep him permanently.

After a while her father drifted off to sleep and her mother motioned her out into the private waiting room next door. As soon as they were there, she pulled her mother into her arms and gave her a big hug.

"What's this for?" she asked.

"Because you look like you need it."

"Oh, I'm fine," she said, waving Louisa's concerns away with the flip of her wrist. "I'm just a little tired. And homesick."

"And worried about Father?"

"Nothing to worry about," she said brightly, but Louisa could hear the undertone of strain in her voice, like guitar strings stretched too taut. "His cardiologist was in yesterday and he's still confident the heart pump will do its job and your father will be back on his feet in no time. We just have to be patient."

A week ago Louisa probably would have believed her, despite all the evidence to the contrary. She would have believed it because it was what she wanted to hear. Now the blinders were off and she was ready to view the world from all sides.

"That's a nice fantasy," Louisa told her. "Now, why don't you tell me what he really said."

She gave her mother credit. She managed to hold it together for a good ten seconds, but then everything in her seemed to let go and she crumbled before Louisa's eyes. In the past that might have scared Louisa to death, but now she just took her mother into her arms and held her while she sobbed her heart out. She stroked her hair and rubbed her back, the way her mother had for Louisa when she was little. When the downpour finally ceased, Louisa handed her a tissue, and as she dabbed her eyes, it seemed as though some of the stress she'd been carrying around had lifted.

"I'm sorry I fell apart like that," she said. "I must look a fright."

"We all need a good cry every now and then. And you look beautiful, as always."

"It's just been a long few weeks. A long few *years,* actually."

"It's not working, is it?" Louisa said. "The pump."

Her mother shook her head. "There should have been a much more drastic improvement since the last time they checked. They could leave him on it, but the longer he stays on, the odds of infection increase. In his weakened state it could be fatal."

"And without the pump?"

"He could live as long as a few years."

But they both knew he probably wouldn't. He didn't have the strength left. Or the will.

"What are the chances he would have another heart attack?" Louisa asked.

"Very likely."

"And the odds he would survive?"

"Slim to none. There's just too much damage already."

"How did he take the news?"

"You know, I think in a way he was…relieved. He's fought so hard. Maybe he feels he finally has an excuse to surrender without letting us down."

"He could never let me down," Louisa told her. Maybe it was partially due to the seed that Anne had planted in her brain, but after seeing his condition and talking with him, she honestly believed that he was ready to let go. It was his time.

The pain she felt when she thought of losing him was indescribable. Like a thousand arrows straight through the heart, yet knowing that he had made peace with the idea of dying was a deep comfort.

She was surprisingly calm when she talked to Garrett that night and explained the situation. Not that she wasn't sad or upset, but crying wouldn't help anyone at this point.

"If you need me, I can be on the next flight to London," Garrett told her more than once. "Just say the word and I'll be there."

It was so tempting to say yes, but she needed to do this alone. To know that she *could*. Because if she could handle this, she figured she could handle just about anything.

After they hung up, she booted up her laptop to research any information she could find about her father's condition. What they could expect to happen near the end. Waiting for her in her mailbox was another message from her pal the Gingerbread Man. It read, Send the old man my regards.

Thirteen

A well of emotions crashed down on Louisa like a tidal wave and she was suddenly so filled with rage, her first instinct was to lob her computer out the window and watch it smash onto the London streets below. She couldn't recall a time in her life when she had ever felt so angry at another human being.

So he knew where she was, *big bloody deal.* These childish little games he was playing were just plain ridiculous. He needed to grow a pair and confront her face-to-face.

Though they had been strictly forbidden from answering his e-mails for fear that it would provoke him, she'd had enough. Maybe they *should* provoke him, draw him out into the open where he could be identified and captured.

She wrote back, You're a coward.

She clicked the send button and it felt good. It gave her a sense of power.

Barely a minute later another e-mail appeared from him. It said, Careful, Lulu. Or Daddy won't be the only one to shuffle loose the mortal coil.

Seeing him use her nickname and what was a very direct threat gave her such a serious case of the creeps that she slammed the computer shut. Maybe replying to him hadn't been such a good idea after all. What if he did lash out? What if someone was hurt? Then it would be completely her fault.

Damn! If only she would think before she acted. She had to stop being so selfish. So quick to fly off the handle.

At the risk of further restricting her already limited freedom, she opened her computer back up and forwarded the e-mail to the head of security at the palace, then she called Chris to give him a heads-up.

"He's a persistent son of a bitch," Chris noted. "How many e-mails is it now, Louisa? Four or five in the past two weeks?"

"But…how did you—"

"I had the feeling you might be less than honest, so I've been monitoring your e-mail."

"My *private* e-mail?"

"Don't worry, security is under strict orders to read only the messages that come from him."

She wanted to scream at him, tell him that he had no right to violate her privacy, but how could she be angry when he was right? She *had* lied to him. And by doing so, she could have been putting everyone in danger. "I can't seem to stop letting you down, can I?" she lamented.

"I noticed that, too."

"I've been so selfish."

"Yes, you have. Although it probably hasn't helped that we've spent the last twenty-seven years sheltering and spoiling you."

"I don't want to be that person anymore, Chris. I'm tired of her. I want to grow up. I want to be responsible."

"I think we would all appreciate that."

She thought about what she had just done and frowned. "However...there is one last really stupid and irresponsible thing I have to confess to first."

"Oh God, what did you do?"

She told him about the e-mail that she sent to the Gingerbread Man.

"That *was* stupid. You know what they said about provoking him. What's the point of keeping all of this security around if we don't bother to listen?"

"Maybe this time they're wrong. What if we *should* be antagonizing him? Maybe we should draw him out so they can catch him."

"You know that's too dangerous."

"I'm beginning to wonder if it might be worth the risk. I mean, how much longer can we live like this, Chris? Constantly on high alert? Somebody has to *do* something."

"We're *all* frustrated, Louisa, but finding him isn't worth risking anyone's safety. You just have to be patient."

But she was tired of being patient. Sweet, patient, obedient—for the most part anyway—Princess Louisa. She was sick to death of her.

All the time they wasted worrying about their stalker

and what he *might* do was time they should spend living life to the fullest.

And from now on, living her life was exactly what she intended to do.

Garrett was bloody exhausted by the time he trudged up the steps and opened his front door Tuesday night. It had been another long, grueling day and all he wanted to do now was change out of his suit, collapse into bed and call Louisa. Hearing her voice had become the highlight of his day. But he looked forward to tomorrow evening, when she would finally return home. That phrase about absence making the heart grow fonder seemed to have some truth to it.

He let himself inside, dropped his briefcase at the foot of the stairs and headed to the kitchen for a drink. From the hallway he could see the light was on, and since the nurse had left more than an hour ago, that meant Ian was still up.

As odd as it was, Garrett had grown a bit fond of not coming home to an empty house. He didn't resent Ian's presence nearly as much as he thought he would. He no longer had the feeling that any second the other shoe was going to fall, or that he would arrive home from work and his house would be cleaned out. In fact, there were times when he actually enjoyed Ian's company.

But tonight, as he stepped into the kitchen, Ian wasn't alone.

"Louisa?"

Grinning brightly, she sat across from Ian at the kitchen table, a half-finished bottle of beer in front of her on the table. "Surprised to see me?"

Without even thinking about what he was doing, he

rounded the table and scooped up Louisa from her chair. She threw her arms around his neck and hugged him, and the stress of the entire day seemed to evaporate into thin air. He set her down and breathed in the scent of her hair and her skin, relished the feel of her body pressed against him. If Ian hadn't been sitting right there, he and Louisa would have been doing a lot more than just embracing.

Louisa on the other hand didn't seem to care that his brother was in the room. She rose up on her toes and pressed her lips to his. It wasn't a passionate kiss, but it wasn't exactly chaste, either. He considered her more of a champagne and caviar kind of woman, but he had to admit that the flavor of the ale on her lips was a major turn-on.

"I thought you weren't coming home until tomorrow," he said.

She grinned up at him. "I missed you. And I thought it would be fun to surprise you. I even made my security detail hide so you wouldn't see them."

They were apparently good at it, because he hadn't had a clue that they were there. "I'm definitely surprised. Have you been here long?"

"Only an hour or so."

"If I had known I would have left work earlier."

"That's okay." She looked over at Ian and smiled. "Your brother and I have been having a very nice chat."

Garrett regarded him curiously. "Oh, have you?"

Ian grinned. "Don't worry, I didn't tell her anything *too* embarrassing."

Or anything having to do with Garrett's ulterior

motives, he hoped. Of course, if he had, Garrett doubted
Louisa would be so happy to see him.

Is this the way it would be from now on? Garrett
always paranoid that something might slip and she
would learn the truth? *And how would she take it?* he
wondered. As far as he was concerned, the only thing
that mattered was the way he felt about her right here.
Right now.

"How long can you stay?"

"I told Chris that I wouldn't be home tonight." She
gestured down the hall and said, "Can we talk upstairs?"
Her expression gave him the feeling something might
be wrong. Maybe Ian had said something.

"Of course."

He shot Ian a questioning look. Ian shrugged, as if to
say, *Don't ask me.*

Louisa smiled at Ian. "It was really nice talking with
you, Ian."

"You, too," Ian said.

"I know everything will work out."

Ian smiled and nodded.

Garrett wondered what that was about, but he was
more concerned with what was on Louisa's mind.
There was something about her tonight. Something…
different.

Maybe it was her clothes. Clothes that for her, he
suddenly noticed as she preceded him up the stairs,
could almost be considered racy. She wore a sleeveless,
fitted top made from a gauzy, pale pink fabric that was
so sheer, he could see the faintest outline of her bra
underneath. She also wore a fitted skirt in a deep fuchsia
that ended at least six inches above her knee, and a pair
of strappy white sandals with a modest heel.

What had happened in London?

"How is your father?" he asked when they reached the top of the stairs.

"He's very...peaceful."

"That's good, right?"

She nodded and followed him into his bedroom. He closed and locked the door, then turned to ask what she wanted to talk about, but before he could she was back in his arms, hugging herself close to him. Because she seemed to need it, he hugged her back.

"I missed you so much," she said. She nuzzled her face against his shirt, her hair catching in the stubble on his chin.

"I missed you, too."

"I did a lot of thinking while I was gone, about us and our future. I used to be so sure about everything, but now everything has changed. I've changed."

"I felt it. The second I saw you I knew something was different."

"I think I grew up."

"When you say everything has changed, do you mean us?"

"I know I said I want to wait until I'm married to make love, but now I'm thinking, maybe I shouldn't."

Making love to Louisa was pretty much all he'd been able to think of lately, but pushing her into something she wasn't ready for would be a mistake. "I thought waiting was important to you."

"It was. It *is*. But what if I was waiting for the wrong thing? What if it's not about the marriage vows?"

"What *is* it about?"

"The way I feel about you. Right now. I'm pretty sure

I love you, Garrett. In fact, I *know* I do. And I want you to be the first."

"I just don't want you to do something you'll regret later." Maybe, in a way, he didn't feel worthy. He didn't deserve something so special.

"Garrett, if we never made love, then something happened and things didn't work out, I would regret it the rest of my life."

"What makes you think it won't work out?"

"The way things have been going in my life lately, I'd be wise not to take anything for granted."

"I want to," he said. "You have no idea how much I want to. But it feels like we're just jumping into this."

"On the contrary, it's all I've been thinking about. This is not a hasty decision on my part."

"Well, maybe *I* need more time."

A quirky grin curled her lips.

"What?" he asked.

"It's just funny. I'm the virgin, and *you* need time. Most men would jump at the chance to defile me."

She was right. And a couple weeks ago, he might have been one of them. But he wasn't that man anymore. And he had her to thank for that. Being with her had forced him to take a good hard look at his life.

He shrugged and remarked, "I guess I'm just not most men."

"And that," she said, reaching up to stroke his cheek, "is why I want to make love to *you*."

"How about a compromise? Right now we don't say yes or no. We just let things progress naturally, and if it happens, it happens."

"I would be willing to compromise," she said. "If it happens, it happens."

Something in her expression, in the impish smile she was wearing, led him to believe it would be happening sooner rather than later.

"Until then there are other things we could do," she continued as she shoved his suit jacket off his shoulders and let it drop to the floor.

"What things?"

"Kissing." She tugged his tie loose and pulled it from around his neck. "And touching."

She unfastened the buttons on his shirt and it hit the floor in seconds flat.

"Are you in some kind of hurry?" he asked.

"I've just been dying to get my hands on you," she admitted. "And this time I want to touch *everything*."

She wasn't going to get an argument from him. He just hoped she understood that she would have to play fair. A tit for a tat—pardon the expression. Or more appropriately, you can touch mine if I can touch yours.

She jerked the hem of his undershirt from the waist of his slacks and he helped her pull it over his head. She looked at his bare chest as though she had been fasting and he was her first meal in months.

"I love your chest," she said, laying her hands on him. "I love all of you, but I think this is my favorite."

She leaned forward and kissed one nipple, then the other, then she licked him. It was hot as hell, but what really turned him on was the look of pure ecstasy on her face as she did it. She looked halfway there already and he hadn't even touched her yet.

She slid her hands down his chest and across his stomach to the waist of his slacks. She undid the button, pulled the zipper down, then hooked her thumbs under the waistband and eased them down, leaving only his boxers resting low on his hips. He was so hard it seemed they barely contained him.

He waited for her to take those off, too, but instead she said, "Why don't you lie down?"

He climbed into bed and reclined with his head against the pillows. He expected her to climb in with him, but instead she pulled her shirt over her head, then reached behind her and unhooked her bra. As soon as that hit the floor, she tugged the skirt, which must have been made of some sort of stretchy material, down her hips and let it drop to the floor. When the score was even, both of them in only their underwear, she climbed on the bed and knelt beside him.

Suddenly Louisa wasn't admiring his chest anymore. Her eyes were glued to his crotch.

"It looks...*big,*" she said.

"Why don't you touch me and find out for yourself?"

Looking excited and nervous all at once, she reached over and laid her hand on him. After a second or two she slid her hand back and forth, up and down the entire length of him. He couldn't begin to count how many women had touched him like this, but he couldn't recall it ever feeling this fantastic. He usually preferred a woman who knew her way around a man's body. At least, he used to. But watching Louisa touch him, knowing she had never touched a man this way before, was one of the hottest things he had ever seen.

"Feels pretty big to me," she confirmed, her eyes, and her hand, never straying from his hard-on. "But just to be sure that I'm making an accurate estimation, maybe I should take off your boxers."

"You're probably right," he agreed.

Looking as though she were about to unwrap a Christmas gift, she took hold of the waistband of his boxers and eased them down. He lifted his hips to help and when she got them to his feet, he kicked them away.

She made a soft sighing sound, as though she liked what she was seeing. For several seconds she just looked, then reached out and tentatively touched him.

"It's not going to bite," he said.

With a wry smile she repeated the question he'd asked only a few minutes ago. "Are you in some kind of hurry?"

Yes and no.

She wrapped her hand around him and squeezed, and Garrett inhaled sharply. Then she started stroking him and he was in ecstasy.

"Is this right?" she asked.

He groaned his approval and his eyes drifted shut.

"I think I was wrong. This is my favorite part of your body."

In that case, he could think of several ways she could show her appreciation, the majority using her mouth. But he knew that would be pushing too far, too fast. It could be weeks, or even months before she was ready for that, or maybe never. Some women just didn't get off on that sort of thing.

No sooner had the thought formed when Louisa leaned over, the ends of her hair tickling his stomach. He thought, *No way, not even possible*. He felt her breath, warm and moist. Then, starting at the base of his erection, with the flat of her tongue, she licked him, moving slowly upward, and when she reached the tip, the sensation was so intense he jerked.

Louisa lifted her head and shot him a curious look.

In a gravelly voice he said, "Sorry. I just wasn't expecting that."

"Should I stop?"

"No!" he said, a bit too forcefully, then added in a much calmer tone, "Not if you don't want to."

She answered him by doing it again, only this time when she reached the tip, she took him into her mouth. Garrett groaned and tangled his fingers through her hair.

Granted, it took a few tries to get the angle and the rhythm right and she got him with her teeth a couple times, but that didn't seem to matter because within minutes he was barely hanging on.

"If you don't stop, you're going to get more than you bargained for," he warned her, and either she didn't know what he meant, or she didn't care, because instead of stopping, she took him deeper in her mouth.

So damned deep that he instantly lost it.

If there was a world record for the fastest, most intense orgasm, Garrett was pretty sure he'd just broken it. When he opened his eyes, Louisa was still on her knees beside him, grinning.

"I've read that there are women who don't like doing that, but I can't imagine why. I thought it was awesome."

He closed his eyes and said a silent prayer of thanks.

"I'm sorry if I was a little awkward," she said.

He couldn't believe she was *apologizing*. Watching Louisa take him in her mouth, knowing he was the first, just might have been the single most erotic experience of his adult life. Although he was sure that eventually she would manage to top that, too.

"I guess there are some things you just can't learn from a book," she said thoughtfully. "Although I'm sure with practice I'll get better."

He honestly didn't think it could get much better, but he wasn't going to argue. "Feel free to practice on me as often as you like."

"Like right now?" she said, an eager gleam in her eyes. He realized she was serious. She would do it again. Right here, right now. As tempted as he was to say yes, he could never be that selfish.

The only thing he wanted right now was to make *her* feel good.

Fourteen

"Let's try something different instead," Garrett told Louisa, and she was disappointed—right up until the instant he put his hand on her knee then slid it up her inner thigh.

"Why don't we switch places," he suggested, so she took his spot against the pillow and he knelt beside her.

He stroked her thighs, starting low, then moving higher each time, until he was barely grazing the edge of her panties with each pass.

"Has anyone ever touched you like this before?" he asked.

"Does it count if I had clothes on?"

"Nope."

"Then I guess not."

"Then I guess no one ever did this, either." He brushed his fingers against the crotch of her panties and it felt so good Louisa moaned and spread her thighs farther apart. She didn't have to feel it to know that she was so wet, she'd soaked right through the lace.

He slipped his fingers under the edge of her panties and Louisa shuddered. He looked up at her and asked, "You shave?"

"Wax, actually."

"Everything?"

She nodded. "I read that some men like that."

He grinned. "I think I'm going to need a better look before I form a definitive conclusion."

So they were going to play *this* game again. "Do what you must."

Still grinning he hooked his fingers under the edge and slowly pulled the panties down and off her feet, then he tossed them over his shoulder and across the room. Was he worried she might try to put them back on? He knelt between her legs, spreading her thighs apart—*far apart*—then he just looked at her, and as he did, he started getting hard again. It excited and thrilled her to know that he was turned on simply by looking at her.

"Well?" she asked.

He shrugged apologetically. "Still not sure."

His erection said otherwise, but okay, she would play along.

"It might help if you touched me," she said, keeping with the script.

His smile turned feral and there was something wicked behind his eyes. "You're right," he conceded. "That would probably work." He scooted closer, then, instead of using his hands, he leaned forward and brushed his lips against her bare mound. It was so not what she expected, so exciting, Louisa gasped and fisted the sheet.

He had strayed from the script by totally reworking the touching scene.

Garrett looked up at her, wearing a mischievous grin.

"You cheated."

"Just keeping things exciting. Did you want me to stop?"

She glared at him.

He shrugged and said, "Just asking."

He leaned forward and kissed her again, then he licked her and she nearly vaulted off the bed.

He shot her another look and opened his mouth to speak and she said, "Ask me if I want to stop and I'll *hurt* you."

She could tell by his grin that she was right, and this time when he lowered his head, she tangled her fingers through his hair, just in case he got the idea that he would stop again.

But this time he didn't stop. He kissed and nibbled, teased her with his tongue, everywhere but the one place that needed to be kissed and nibbled and teased the most. He drove her to the point of mindless frustration, every muscle coiled so blasted tight she felt like a spring ready to snap.

She shifted her hips, trying to align his mouth just right, but went left when he would go right, and he ended up on the complete opposite side from where he was supposed to be. He got fed up with all of her wiggling and used his weight to pin her against the mattress. She realized the only way to get her point across was to just come right out and tell him.

She opened her mouth to give him a gentle pointer, when suddenly he found her center, and the word she'd been forming came out like a garbled moan. He took her into his mouth and the spring gave its final stretch then snapped like a dry twig, then it sparked and ignited, and burst into flames.

Louisa was still gasping for breath when Garrett flopped down next to her on his side and said, "I'm sorry if I was a little awkward."

She laughed weakly and gave him a playful shove. "You're making fun of me."

He smiled and pushed back a lock of hair that had fallen across her cheek. "Yep."

"What you really need is a geography lesson."

He frowned. "Geography of what?"

"The female anatomy."

He looked confused, then he realized what she meant and laughed. "Is that what all that squirming was for?"

"I was trying to help. You kept missing the target. Though for the life of me, I don't know how. It's right there in the middle."

"Did it ever occur to you that I might have been missing it for a reason?"

"To do what? *Torture* me?"

His grin said that was exactly what he was doing. "You can't tell me you didn't enjoy it."

She could, but it would be a lie.

"I guess I see your point." She rolled close and snuggled up against him, laying her head on his chest, touching him. She just couldn't seem to get close enough, get enough of her hands on his skin. It just felt so…good. But she still wanted more.

She used to hear girls talk about saving themselves

for marriage, and a month or two later admit that they'd given in and slept with their boyfriend. She never got why they didn't just wait. But now, for the first time in her life, she understood. All the kissing and touching and orgasms in the world wouldn't satiate this yearning to be closer to him. To be connected in a way she never had been before.

"I can hardly believe that I'm twenty-seven and I've never been in bed with a naked man before," she said.

"Well, technically, neither have I. But you don't hear me bragging about it."

She laughed and tickled his ribs, making him squirm.

He batted her hand away. "Don't do that."

"Why, are you ticklish?"

He frowned. "I refuse to answer that on the grounds that it might incriminate me."

She waited a minute or two, then did a sneak attack on his belly and he nearly jumped out of his skin. There was nothing more adorable than a big, tough man who was ticklish.

His tone stern, he said, "*Don't,* Louisa."

Two minutes ago didn't he admit to deliberately torturing her? And he thought she would cut him any slack?

She dove for his armpit, but he was too quick. He captured her wrists and rolled her onto her back, pinning her to the mattress with the weight of his body, and just like that, they were back in the position they had been in the other day, his erection cradled between her legs, only this time there were no clothes to get in the way. This time it was just skin against skin.

Just like before they both went completely still and Garrett got that *what-have-I-done* look.

"If it happens, it happens," she reminded him, but they both seemed to realize that, ready or not, it was happening.

In an odd way, she sort of felt as if she was the veteran and he was the virgin, which certainly put an interesting spin on things.

She pulled free of his grasp, wrapped her arms around his neck and kissed him. For a while that was all they did...kissed and touched, and it was really...*sweet*. But she didn't want sweet. She wanted sexy and crazy and out of control. Grinding and thrusting and writhing in ecstasy. She was *aching* for it. But every time she tried to move things along, he shut her down. If she tried to touch his erection, he would intercept her hand and put it on his chest instead. If she tried to kiss his throat or nibble his ear, he would duck out of the way. It was almost as if, the instant he realized where this was going, he'd switched off emotionally. Now she was feeling more frustrated than aroused.

She slipped her hand down from his shoulder, and when she hit the fleshy part just below his underarm, she gave it a good, hard pinch.

"Ow!" He jerked his arm away and looked at the red mark she'd created. "What was that for?"

"I thought you might enjoy actually feeling something."

His expression softened. "Louisa, what are you talking about? Of course I feel something."

She shrugged. "I couldn't tell."

"I'm just taking it slow."

"I noticed." At the rate he was going, she would be

eighty before they finally made love. "I have an idea. Let's pretend I'm not a virgin. Make love to me like you would if this wasn't my first time."

"But it is, and I don't want to hurt you."

"Maybe I want you to hurt me. I'd rather feel pain than feel *nothing!*"

Anger sparked in his eyes and she thought, *good, at least he's feeling something.* Now that she had her foot in the door, rather than back down, she stoked the fire.

"Do you even want this, Garrett?"

"You know that I do," he growled.

"Then bloody well act like it or stop wasting my time!"

Garrett stared down at Louisa, his temper blazing, unable to believe what he'd just heard her say. What had happened to his sweet, innocent princess?

Good riddance to her, he thought. He liked this Louisa better anyway. She had spunk and passion. This Louisa, the one who was now unflinchingly meeting his eye, unwilling to back down until he realized what an ass he was being, would never bore him.

She was right, he was trying like hell not to feel this, because he knew deep down that once he made love to her, once he accepted the gift that she offered with no question or reserve, every one of his defenses would crumble. He might be taking her virginity, but in exchange she would be taking from him something even more remarkable. The love in a heart he believed he had locked away for good.

If passion was what she wanted, that's what he would give her.

He wrapped a hand under the back of her neck,

lifted her head right off the pillow and crushed his lips to hers. If he startled her, she didn't let it show. She moaned against his lips and wrapped herself around him, pressing her body to his.

Everything they had done up to now, all the kissing and touching, had been child's play. Right here, right now, this was the real thing. He held nothing back, and neither did she. Her ability to give herself so freely, with no shame or hesitation, never ceased to amaze him.

Her body language said she was more than ready, and he could only endure so much of her writhing around underneath him. He was considering warning her first, so she could prepare herself before he took the plunge, but he never got the chance. He rocked against her and as he did, she arched up, by some fluke of nature creating the perfect angle, and the next thing he knew, he was inside her.

Louisa's eyes went wide and she gasped softly, her mouth forming a perfect *O,* and he imagined he was wearing a similar expression.

"Did you mean to do that?" she asked.

He shook his head. "It just…happened."

Was it fate? She had talked about that often during their phone conversations while she was in London, how she used to believe in it, but now she wasn't so sure. He never believed in things like fate and Karma, but the ease of their bodies coming together in what seemed to be perfect sync, could that really be an accident? *Everything* about their relationship seemed somehow… predisposed.

"You're all the way in, right?" Louisa asked.

"As far as I can go." And she was tight. Tight and wet and warm. And wonderful.

She blinked, looking adorably confused, and asked, "When is it going to hurt?"

"Actually, if it was going to, I think it would have already." *Now can we please get on with it?*

"But it's *supposed* to," she insisted.

Well, that had to be a first, a virgin who *wanted* sex to hurt.

"I don't know what to tell you," he said.

She opened her mouth to say something, and before she got a word out, he covered her lips with his and kissed her. Not so easy for her to talk with his tongue in her mouth.

He started to move inside her, slow and easy, savoring the sensation of slippery walls hugging him so tightly, knowing that at this rate he would be lucky to last five minutes.

Louisa sighed against his lips, tunneled her fingers through his hair, looking as though she was in pure ecstasy. It took all of his concentration, and a little extra he didn't even know he had, to keep up the slow, steady pace.

Louisa pushed at his chest, saying, "I want to see."

He leaned back and braced himself up on his arms, increasing the friction and giving all new meaning to the word *torture*. He could barely watch as Louisa rose up on her elbows, spreading her legs wide so to gaze at the place where their bodies were joined.

"That's us," she whispered, her face flushed, her eyes glazed and full of wonder. "You're inside me, Garrett."

If she was going to give him a play-by-play, he wouldn't last five seconds. He was barely hanging on as it was, then Louisa's head rolled back and her body began to tremble with release, clamping down around him, squeezing and contracting until he lost it, too, riding out the crest of the wave with her.

Louisa was no longer a virgin.

She always thought that afterward she would feel different somehow, that anyone who looked at her would just *know*. But as she and Garrett lay wrapped around each other, arms and legs entwined, she didn't really feel any different. There was something else she didn't feel, either. Regret.

Wait a minute…had they…?

"Garrett?"

"Hmm," he mumbled sleepily.

"Did we…*forget* something?" she asked. "When we made love?"

"If we did, it's going to have to wait, because I need to sleep for a while."

"Garrett, did we use birth control?"

He was quiet for a minute, like he was scanning the memory banks, then he mumbled a curse.

She cringed. "Should I take that as a no?"

"Maybe I was thinking you had it covered, or maybe I just *wasn't* thinking. I don't know."

"My period is due any second, so odds are that I'm not fertile, but there's no guarantee."

He nodded and yawned. "Okay."

She untangled herself from him and sat up. "You're not worried?"

He pried one eye open and peered up at her. "Didn't you just tell me not to be?"

"I also said there's no guarantee."

He shrugged. "So we'll wait and see."

"That's it?"

"I don't see what you're so worried about," he grumbled. "Aren't you the one who said you want sixteen kids?"

"I didn't say sixteen, I said *six*. And yes, of course I want kids. But I also don't want to get you stuck in a situation you don't want to be in."

"You won't."

"How can you know that?"

"Because I know."

"But *how?*"

Garrett pushed himself up on his elbows and rubbed his eyes with his thumb and forefinger. "Okay, I was going to wait and do this right, with a nice candlelit dinner and maybe some soft music playing. But if it'll ease your mind, and you don't mind that I haven't gotten the ring yet, or the fact that I'm too bloody tired to get on one knee, I could ask you to marry me right now."

She bit her lip, to hold back the huge smile that was just dying to get out. He wanted to *marry* her.

"No, that's okay," she said. "I can wait."

"Does that mean I can sleep now?"

"Of course."

He collapsed back down and closed his eyes. Unfortunately, she wasn't the least bit tired. She had just lost her virginity and Garrett had more or less proposed to her. How could she even think of sleeping? Not to mention that there was the slightest possibility that she could be *pregnant!* If she was, her baby would be close in age to the triplets. Who could be born very soon.

"Garrett?" she said softly.

He groaned.

"Sorry. I just wondered if you would mind me using your computer. I wanted to look online for some gifts for the babies, since getting out to shop these days is complicated, to say the least."

He nodded and grumbled something incoherent.

"Thanks!" She pressed a kiss to his cheek and rolled out of bed. Since she didn't feel like getting dressed, she found a robe hanging on the back of his closet door and slipped it on. She thought about going downstairs and making herself a cup of tea, but Ian was camped out on the family-room couch and she didn't want to disturb him.

Garrett's office was across the hall at the opposite end, and typically male. Lots of glass and steel and hundreds of books. She'd never realized what an avid reader he must be. But she had pulled a few strings and discovered that he had graduated at the top of his class at both primary school and university. She hoped their children would inherit his intelligence. Not that she was a dummy. Louisa had done all right in school. Her problem was that she just didn't care.

Louisa doesn't work to her potential became her slogan for the better part of her childhood.

She made herself comfortable in Garrett's chair and when she touched the mouse, the computer screen flashed to life. His e-mail program was open and she was about to click it closed when she saw a list of e-mails with the subject: Princess Louisa. They had been sent back and forth between Garrett and someone named Weston. She noticed the oldest one dated back to the weekend of the charity ball. Had it really been less than three weeks ago? It felt as though she had known him forever.

Garrett probably wrote about meeting her, and how

magical it had been. Not that he would have used the term *magical,* but something equivalent in guy speak.

Louisa knew firsthand what it was like to have someone shuffling through her personal messages, and realized how wrong it would be to invade his privacy, but she was *dying* to know what he'd said about her.

Maybe if she just took a quick peek. Just the first one, and that was it.

She clicked it open, and as she expected, it was about her. But the more she read, she realized it had nothing to do with meeting her at the ball, and the things he'd written were never meant for her eyes. And as she clicked open one message after the other, it only got worse. She felt sick to her stomach and sick in her heart, and she finally had to face the realization that her family had been right about her all along. It was as though destiny had painted a target on her back that announced: *Use me! I'm dense and naive!*

A lot of men had taken aim and missed, but Garrett, the man she thought she would spend the rest of her life with, had hit the target dead on. He had her totally duped. And if she'd only been paying attention, if she'd bothered to look hard enough, maybe she would have noticed the arrow planted in her back.

Fifteen

Garrett jerked out of a sound sleep and bolted up in bed. He reached over to feel for Louisa, but the sheets were cold.

He'd been dreaming about his computer, about Louisa asking to use it. Or had that really happened?

They had talked about birth control, then he'd started dozing....

Yes. She'd asked to use it to shop for baby things.

Then he realized why he'd been jolted awake. He had closed his e-mail program, hadn't he?

He flung back the covers and groped around the floor for his slacks. If not, would she have noticed the e-mails with her name in the subject? And if she noticed them, would she have read them?

He yanked his pants on and was out the bedroom door before he even got them fastened. He half ran down the hall to his office and burst through the door, but he knew the second he saw her sitting there, her face ashen, that not only had she seen the e-mails, she'd read them, too.

Bloody goddamn hell.

Why hadn't he just erased them? Why leave evidence? Unless he actually wanted to get caught. Was living with the guilt of the way he had planned to use her too much to bear? And it was all there, every gruesome detail.

For what felt like an eternity he just stood there, at a loss for what to say. At a time like this, *I'm sorry* didn't even begin to cover it.

Finally she looked up at him and said in a very calm voice, "Everything my family has said, about me being too trusting and naive, I guess they were right."

"Louisa—"

"You and this Weston fellow must have had a good laugh at my expense. I mean, I fell for it, hook, line and sinker, didn't I? You had me totally duped."

"If you would just let me explain—"

"Explain what?" She gestured to the screen. "It's all right here. I've read each one at least a dozen times, so I'll never forget how stupid I've been."

The idea that she could believe he was that man, the one who had been so selfishly obsessed, made him sick. Why didn't she scream at him and call him names? Instead she sounded so...disappointed.

Anger he could handle, but this? This was...*awful.* It was heart wrenching and painful. It wasn't the first time he'd let someone down, but Louisa didn't deserve this.

"That's not me," he said. "Not anymore. I don't even recognize that man."

"People don't change, isn't that what you told me? You can't have it both ways."

She was using his own words against him. And could he blame her? He'd painted himself into this corner.

"I was an ass, I admit it. I was greedy and selfish, and yes, I used you, and I will never be able to adequately express how sorry I am for that. But then everything... changed. The money and the power, none of that matters to me now. *You* are the only thing that matters."

"I don't believe you. This is all just a game to you. I think you're just sorry that you lost, and you would do or say anything to get what you want." She shrugged and said, "What the hell, I should be thanking you. You've given me a gift, Garrett. You've finally made me see things clearly. See people for who they are. My family spent all those years sheltering me, but you gave me what I really needed. You've taught me how not to trust."

Her honesty, her ability to trust people enough to always say exactly what was on her mind, was what made her special and different from everyone else. And what she was telling him now was that he had killed that. He'd made her less than whole.

The idea that he had done that to her was almost too much to comprehend. No man should have that kind of power over another human being. Especially a man like him. And he would do anything, *anything* it took to turn the clock back, but there was no way to fix this. No way to repair the damage he'd done.

"I should go now," she said rising to her feet, wearing his robe. She walked past him to the door, but stopped halfway through and looked back. "Just so you know,

I don't regret that we made love. It doesn't make sense, but despite everything, I'm still glad it was you."

If she would hit him or cry or show some sort of emotion, he wouldn't feel so rotten. He would at least know that she cared. And as long as she cared there was still a chance. But her eyes looked…dead. The spark was gone.

He stood there listening as she dressed and gathered her things from his room and walked down the stairs. He heard the front door open, and hushed conversation between Louisa and her bodyguards. Then, when he heard it close, he had to fight to keep from going after her.

He wanted to beg her to stay. He wanted to tell her that without her in it, his life meant nothing.

But maybe without him around to poison her soul she would recover. Maybe someday she would be herself again.

It was no longer about what he wanted or needed. This was about Louisa. And the kindest thing he could do for her now was let her go.

On autopilot, Garrett walked down to the kitchen and made himself a cup of tea, then sat at the table, cupping the steaming mug in his hands, trying to chase away the chill that had settled in his bones.

He was still sitting there when Ian hobbled in, hours after the tea had gone cold.

Ian saw Garrett's wrinkled pants and robe, and with one brow lifted said, "Must have been some night. You're usually off to the gym by now."

"What time is it?" Garrett asked, but his voice was so rusty he had to clear his throat.

"After eight. Louisa still sleeping?"

"She left last night."

Ian limped to the stove and put the kettle on. "Sorry to hear that. She mentioned something about making crepes for breakfast. Maybe another time."

"There won't be another time."

Ian turned to him, frowning. "What do you mean?"

"I messed up. I lost her."

Ian turned the kettle off and crossed the kitchen, easing into the chair across from Garrett. "Give her a day or two to cool down. It's probably not as bad as it seems."

If only it were that simple. "No, it's pretty bad."

"Something to do with that plan your mate Wes mentioned?"

Since Garrett no longer had to worry about the truth getting out, he told Ian the entire grisly tale, right up to the confrontation in his office.

Ian winced. "Ah, you gotta hate it when they lay on the guilt. Women do love their drama."

"Louisa doesn't have a manipulative bone in her body."

"Don't misunderstand. I'm not suggesting she's doing it on purpose. Women just open their mouths and out it comes. They don't even realize it's happening."

"You didn't see her face. Her eyes. I think she honestly has no feelings left for me whatsoever."

"Take it from someone who's been in his share of relationships—she does. Besides, I've seen the way she looks at you. That woman loves you."

"Even if she does, I don't think I deserve her. Even if I could get her back, which seems bloody unlikely at this point, I'd always worry that I might screw up and disappoint her again."

"And you will. But so will she."

Somehow he couldn't imagine Louisa ever making a mistake. Other than trusting him.

"You love her, don't you?" Ian asked, and Garrett nodded. "Did you tell her?"

"I couldn't."

"Why the hell not?"

"Because she wouldn't have believed me. She would have thought I was saying it to try to win her back."

Ian nodded grimly. "Good point. It's confusing as hell, isn't it? Being in love. It's like you lose a part of yourself, but at the same time, you gain so much back."

"You sound as though you're speaking from experience."

Ian rubbed his palms together, his brow wrinkled. "I guess now is as good a time as any to tell you."

"Tell me what?"

"Though I appreciate all you've done for me, I'm going to be leaving soon."

"Where are you going?"

"Remember the girl I told you about? Maggie?"

"The farmer's daughter?" Garrett asked, and Ian nodded.

"Well, her father has offered to make me a partner in his cattle business. I've just been waiting for my leg to stabilize enough to travel."

"Why would he do that?"

"Because I'm going to be the father of his grand-child."

Garrett's jaw fell. He tried to come up with an appropriate response, but he was too flabbergasted to speak.

"Hard to believe, I know. *Me,* someone's papa."

"How long have you known?"

"A while. We found out a few weeks before her father chased me off. Maggie and I have been communicating behind her father's back ever since I left. We've been planning to run away together, but we needed money. That's why I took your car. I was going to sell it. But as I was driving away, I felt so damned guilty. Which of course was an odd sensation for me, seeing as how I never feel guilty. I really was bringing it back. I was going to tell you the truth and ask for your help. I was going to beg you for a job and maybe a small parcel of land to get started. A loan I could pay back over time."

"So why didn't you tell me the truth?"

"After the accident, I knew you would never believe me. I knew I would have to prove myself to you. As soon as I was able to work, I was going to get Maggie and bring her back here, but her parents found out she was pregnant and now they want me to come live with them instead." He leaned forward. "I know changing won't be easy, but I'm determined to try. I want to do right by my child. I won't make the mistakes our father made."

Garrett clasped his brother's hand. "Then you'll be a damned fine father. And a good man."

Ian gave his hand a squeeze then quickly turned away, but not before Garrett saw what looked like a tear spill from his eye. Ian got up from his chair and hobbled over to the stove to put on the kettle. "Might as well get comfortable. We have work to do."

"What kind of work?"

Ian turned to him and grinned. "We're going to figure out a way to get your princess back."

Louisa wanted to cry, but the tears wouldn't come. She wanted to scream and throw things, but she couldn't work up the will to feel angry. She wanted to hate Garrett for being so cold and calculating, for lying to her, but she couldn't make herself hate him.

The only emotion she had been able to feel was disgust. Disgust in herself, for letting this happen. For being so unsuspecting and so blind.

She'd come home from Garrett's in a daze and had gone straight to her room. She stood there for several minutes, looking around, really seeing it. The frilly pink curtains and canopy bed, the doll collection lining the wall. She was twenty-seven years old and she was living in a little girl's room.

Disgusted with herself, she shoved it all into trash bags. First thing the next morning, she picked up the phone and called a decorator. She didn't tell anyone or ask anyone's permission. She just did it, and surprisingly, no one seemed to care.

"You can't stay like this," Anne told her a few days later. She was the only one Louisa had confided in. She just couldn't bear facing the rest of them yet, knowing how disappointed they would be in her and how all this time they had been right.

"Stay like what?" she asked Anne.

"So unhappy. Without you to cheer me up and your

glass-half-full mentality, I could very possibly sink into a bottomless pit of negativity."

Louisa didn't want the responsibility any longer. She was sick of trying to convince herself and everyone else that everything was roses and sunshine. She wanted to start living in the real world. She even wondered, since she had never actually experienced real, soul-deep grief before, if this funk she had slipped into, this abyss of nothingness, was just her peculiar way of coping. She'd even stopped caring about the Gingerbread Man, who it would seem had slipped under the radar.

Five days after she and Garrett had split up, Louisa was in a meeting with her decorator finalizing the plans for her new room when Chris popped his head in. He was usually at the hospital with Melissa, so it was a pleasant surprise to see him. "Is this a bad time?"

"Not at all—we're just finishing up."

"In that case, why don't you come to the study? There's someone I want you to meet."

"Who?"

"A friend."

Curious as to who this mystery friend could be, she said goodbye to the decorator and followed Chris down the hall to the study. She followed him in, and when she saw the man standing by the window, dressed in jeans, a polo shirt and Docksiders, she froze.

"Louisa, this is a good friend of mine, Garrett Sutherland, and Garrett, meet my sister Princess Louisa."

Garrett walked slowly toward her, one hand tucked into his pants pockets, the other holding a thick legal-size manila envelope, and for the first time in days she finally felt something.

Confusion.

It must have shown on her face, because Garrett said, "I thought we should be reintroduced, since the man you met the first time, at the ball, wasn't really me."

Louisa looked at Chris, who didn't seem to find it the least bit unusual that he was reintroducing her to the man who, as far as he knew, she was planning to marry.

"He knows everything," Garrett explained. "I figured it would be best to come clean with everyone."

"Well, I've done my part," Chris told Garrett. "I'll leave you to it."

The idea of being alone with Garrett made Louisa's heart jump into her throat. "Leave you to what?"

"Win you back," Garrett declared, looking so confident it was unsettling. That night when he'd found her reading the e-mails, he had looked so beside himself, so at a loss for what to do or say, it had been empowering. It had given her the strength to do what she had to. She wasn't feeling quite so confident now.

"You can't have me," she told him.

"If you're so sure about that, then what's the harm in hearing me out?" He paused then added, "Unless you're afraid."

She wasn't afraid—she was *terrified*. But she couldn't let it show, because men like him fed off fear. "Fine," she said, walking to the sofa, remembering halfway there that it was where they had sat together his first time here, so she changed course for the chair instead. She sat primly on the edge, arms folded over her chest. "Say what you have to say. Even though it will be a waste of time."

"First," he began, taking a seat on the sofa and setting the envelope beside him, "I want to thank you."

Thank her? "For what?"

"For reading those e-mails. You needed to know the truth, and God knows I never would have had the guts to tell you myself. The fear of you someday finding out and of what it would do to us would have haunted me for the rest of my life."

She didn't know what to say to that, but he didn't seem to expect her to say anything.

"Second, for the record, as far as lies go, I only lied to you twice. And before you go saying that a lie by omission is still a lie," he continued, which was exactly what she'd been about to do, "you have to admit that it's at the very least a slippery slope, because *no one* says everything they're thinking one hundred percent of the time. And while I may not have always been forthcoming about my intentions, I was always honest. Except those two times."

"One was about your brother, right?"

"Right."

"So what was the other one?"

"No man, especially one with my past dating habits, forgets to use a condom."

Her jaw dropped. "You did that on *purpose?* Why? So I would *have* to marry you? And isn't it typically the woman who traps the man?"

He grinned, his dimple winking at her, and her knees went soft. "It had nothing to do with trapping you. It was more of a base instinct thing. My way of branding you or possessing you or something."

She frowned. "I'm pretty sure the last man to act on that particular instinct wore animal skins and carried a club."

"Nope. Men still do it. And if they don't, they want to. It's nature."

She didn't know if she was buying that.

"And, quite frankly, it feels better," he admitted, and she thought that sounded like a much more plausible excuse.

"But back to my original point. I lied twice. That's it."

Okay, fine, so he wasn't a liar. That didn't mean he wasn't a lot of other awful things that she wanted nothing to do with.

"Okay, third," he said, "for all the times in my life that I told myself I didn't give a damn what my father thought of me, I was still trying to impress him. To show him that he was wrong about me. And unfortunately, that desire manifested itself in an overdeveloped sense of greed and entitlement. Coincidentally, all the things you claimed to hate in men. I guess I was just good at hiding it."

"So, Daddy made you do it?" she snapped, and instantly felt guilty for the heartless comment. She was just no good at being snarky.

But Garrett didn't look wounded. "Don't misunderstand. It's not an excuse. What I did was wrong and inexcusable. It's only an explanation of why I acted that way."

"Do you still care?"

"What my father thinks?" He regarded her curiously, as though he'd never really considered it before. "I suppose I'll always care somewhere deep down, or at the very least, wish things were different. The difference is, now I know that the things my father said and did were his problem. They had nothing to do with me."

So, unresolved past family issues were always a nuisance, and she was glad that he'd finally made peace with it, but it had nothing to do with her. And it certainly didn't mean she could trust him.

"Okay, fourth, and this one is important so you need to really pay attention. You are *not* stupid or naive. In fact, you're one of the smartest, most resourceful people I know." He leaned forward, meeting her eye. "When I met you, Louisa, I was in a dark place. I had sunk about as low as I could go, but despite that, you saw the good in me. The *real* me that was trapped underneath all the lies. By putting your trust in me, you drew me back out into the light. You *saved* me. You also made me realize what's important." He picked up the envelope. "And it isn't this."

He held it out to her, and only when she took it did she realize her hands were trembling. Her heart was pounding, too. So hard it felt as if it might beat right through her chest.

"What's in here?" she asked.

"The deed to every parcel of land I own on both Thomas and Morgan Isle. Everything I own. Except my father's land. That one I want to keep."

He was going to sell his land?

"Of course, the names will have to be legally transferred," he explained. "But as far as I'm concerned, they're yours now."

"*Mine?* You're *giving* it to me?"

"Consider it an early wedding gift."

"But what if I won't marry you?"

He shrugged. "Then just consider it a gift."

"But…Garrett, this is your livelihood. Everything you've worked so hard for. You can't just give it away."

"I just did."

"But—"

"Louisa, I would rather be penniless than *ever* be that man again."

"But…what will you do?"

He shrugged. "Who knows, maybe I'll try farming."

God, he was serious. He was going to give up everything for her. But not just for her, for himself. *Everything.*

This was crazy.

No, this was Garrett. The real Garrett. The one she had fallen in love with. And *still* loved.

"Well," he said, rising from the couch, "that was pretty much all I came here to say. I won't take up any more of your time."

He made a move toward the door, and Louisa launched herself at him. She didn't even know she was going to do it until she was on her feet. But she knew, deep down to the depths of her soul, that she couldn't let him go. Not ever. And when his arms went around her and he held her close, all the emotions she thought might have shut down forever came rushing back at the same time.

It was a little overwhelming, and even a little scary, but it was wonderful.

Garrett buried his face in her hair, nuzzled her neck. "I love you so much, Louisa."

"I love you, too."

"As long as we both shall live?"

She squeezed him tighter. "Definitely. Even longer."

"I have a ring in my pocket with your name on it, and if you would let go for a second, I'll even get down on one knee."

Instead of letting go, she held him tighter. "The ring can wait. This can't."

For a long time they just held each other, and Louisa thought about marriage and babies and loving only him for the rest of her life, and she started having another feeling, one she was sure both she and Garrett would be feeling a lot from now on.

Happy.

* * * * *

And the ROYAL SEDUCTIONS *continue
with Anne's story,*
EXPECTANT PRINCESS, UNEXPECTED AFFAIR,
*coming next month
from Silhouette Desire.*

COMING NEXT MONTH

Available August 10, 2010

#2029 HONOR-BOUND GROOM
Yvonne Lindsay
Man of the Month

#2030 FALLING FOR HIS PROPER MISTRESS
Tessa Radley
Dynasties: The Jarrods

#2031 WINNING IT ALL
"Pregnant with the Playboy's Baby"—Catherine Mann
"His Accidental Fiancée"—Emily McKay
A Summer for Scandal

#2032 EXPECTANT PRINCESS, UNEXPECTED AFFAIR
Michelle Celmer
Royal Seductions

#2033 THE BILLIONAIRE'S BABY ARRANGEMENT
Charlene Sands
Napa Valley Vows

#2034 HIS BLACK SHEEP BRIDE
Anna DePalo